PLAY ME

A ROCK CHAMBER BOYS NOVEL

~ BOOK ONE ~

Copyright © 2017 Daisy Allen
Play Me: A Rock Chamber Boys Novel
By Daisy Allen
All rights reserved.
Printed 2019.

This book may not be reproduced, scanned, or distributed in any printed or electronic form without permission from the author. Please do not participate in or encourage piracy of copyrighted materials in violation of the author's rights. All characters and storylines are the properties of the author and your support and respect is appreciated.

This book is a work of fiction. The characters and events portrayed in this book are fictitious. Any similarity to real persons, living or dead, is coincidental and not intended by the author.

*For everyone who ever played me a song just
because they thought I'd like it.
I did.
Thank you.*

Music is everything.

*And for my father and husband;
Infinitely patient
and
Infinitely supportive.*

PROLOGUE

Sometimes the noise is so loud that for a moment everything goes quiet.

Just for a moment.

An eerie second of complete silence.

A breath of time for the ears to reset themselves.

And then the sounds explode back into life.

The screams from the crowd, the boom from the speakers, the scratches of my cello on the floor, my bandmates' grunts and heavy breaths of exertion as we bring our music, our passion to life.

A million different sounds melding into a complete and utter perfection of cacophony.

There's almost nothing that can compare with being on stage and being completely engulfed by the magnificence of music and man coming together.

Almost.

She once said that the only thing that mattered was the band.

She was right.

Was.

Now the only thing that matters is her.

CHAPTER ONE

SEBASTIAN

"Sebastian! Over here!"

I turn at the sound of my name and a paparazzo's camera flash explodes in my face.

"Argh, fuck it!" I throw up a hand to cover my eyes and pull the sunglasses down from my head. "I don't mind the picture taking but do they have to bloody blind me?" I turn and say to my assistant, Hank, who throws me an unsympathetic look.

"Oh yes, poor you. Poor wittle musician eyeballs hurt by the wittle fwash."

The look I give him is nowhere near as withering as I hope – I know this because his reaction is to double over in laughter.

"For god's sake, hurry up, boys," a voice admonishes us from behind. Our manager, Dennis, looks over at us, like he's wondering for the hundredth time why he chose this job that's the equivalent of babysitting a group of full-grown boy infants.

"Yes, boys, hurry up now. Hup, two, three, four!" Jez runs up between us, mimicking Dennis and throwing his arms over our shoulders, pushing us forward. "These Aussie babes aren't going to wait forever now!"

We push through the hordes of people, half our own and half annoyed fellow travelers just trying to get home. We wave and grin gratefully at the crowd of smiling faces of fans greeting us as we walk to the exit, where our SUVs are also waiting for us.

"Sebastian! Jez! Marius! Brad!" The crowd kicks up into the familiar chant of our names.

Jez turns to grin at me after winking at a cute, perky blonde obviously vying for his attention. "Welcome to the land down under indeed. I think I'm going to like it here."

I elbow him in the ribs and he faux cries out. "Just don't be liking it too much. We have to go back to gay Paris someday," I remind him.

"Not until my skin is brown and my butt crack is filled with sand." And before I can stop him, he's pulled out of the safety of our body-guarded entourage and off to flirt with the blonde standing behind the barricade.

"You got everything, Seb?" Hank asks me, taking my leather laptop bag from me and putting it in the backseat of my assigned car.

"Yeah, bro. Except, I think I forgot to pack some new rosin before we left. I used it all up during the last practice." I take a look around to see everyone else getting into their cars and I fold myself into the backseat of mine, moving over so Hank can get in behind me.

"We can pick some up on the way to sound check, boss."

"Stop calling me that, you're my nephew," I snap at him.

"Fine. UNCLE." He emphasizes the word, knowing I hate how it makes me feel old.

"Stick with 'boss', you little prick."

He laughs and he sounds just like my brother used to and the veins in my chest tug on my heart just a bit.

"To the Shangri-La Hotel, please," he says to the driver.

As the car cruises forward, we lean back, sinking into the soft, butter-like leather and grin at each other, wondering how we'd gotten so lucky to have ended up here.

CADENCE

"You're killing me here, George." I tell the shop owner, not for the first time.

"Hey, you told me to tell you-..." he starts to defend himself.

I cut him off, "I know, but I have to work to a budget. A tiny ant's bladder-sized budget at that."

"Fine, give them back then." He reaches for the stack of newly arrived sheet music and I pull out of reach, hugging them to my chest.

"Just let me...sniff them a bit?" I bury my face in the paper, inhaling the fresh ink scent of the thin lines and little black notes.

"You'd think I'd be used to musicians after owning this store for thirty-five years, but you crazies get more bonkers as the years go by. Fine, sniff all you like." He turns back to his ancient register, glaring at the buttons as if willing them to work with the power of his mind.

I can't help but grin at him over the top of the stack of music clenched in my hand. I bought my first piano book from this very store, from George, twenty-one years ago. And even now, as a music teacher, it's here I come for all my supplies. This small, dark and dingy little music store, packed to the brim with all and any supplies you could possibly need. George can tell what you need the second that little bell on his door dings, and will make sure you get the right equipment. As he said, musicians are a crazy bunch and as unique and sensitive as snowflakes, and what works for one, may not work for another.

I put down the sheet music, resigned to the fact that the school can't afford any more this month and wander to the back of the store just as the door clangs open and a group of young men barge in, talking loudly, disrupting the quiet sanctity of the store that I love so much.

I can barely make out what they're saying, with as many accents among them as there are bodies. They head to the register and through the shelf stacks I can count 1...2...3 of them. They ask George something and I hear him explode into laughter. I scrunch up my nose and slink deeper into the store, annoyed that their loud banter is interrupting my happy browsing time.

Skimming over the list of things I need for my class, I head for the strings section.

The sound of laughter from the front of the store drifts down to the little corner in the back. I can't help but smile to myself as I just make out George's voice, three against one, and he's still out-talking them.

"Pirazzi...pirazzi..." I scour the shelf for my preferred brand of cello rosin. There it is. On sale! And only one jar left. I reach out for it.

Then a white, painful spark zaps my fingers and travels all the way down my body.

CHAPTER TWO

SEBASTIAN

"Ow! What the flying fuck!" I snap my hand back, shaking it in a vain attempt to ease the sting. It's too late, my whole body feels invigorated as the electric spark that zapped my fingertips is still making its way along every nerve of my body.

But I honestly don't think it's from the static.

I think it's because of the adorable, curvy brunette standing in front of me. And glaring.

"What?" I ask, rather discourteously, out of a very unfamiliar feeling of nervousness. I think I'm squirming a little under her unwavering stare. I would've guessed that it was because she recognized me, but it's definitely not a look of adoration. Her large, hot chocolate brown eyes obviously don't give a fuck who I am.

"There's no need to swear. I didn't bite you, it was just a little spark." She dresses me down in one sentence, still not looking away and I squirm a little more.

"Geez, what are you, a freakin' kindergarten teacher?" I try to deflect. Then immediately feel bad. As if I don't want her to hate me. Though I'm not sure 3why should I even care?

"Why?" she answers my question with a question, those beautiful, moon-shaped orbs still fixed on me. It's almost hypnotic.

I shrug and force myself to tear my eyes from hers. Their effect isn't lessened however. Who is this woman? I can't figure out if I'm scared of her or attracted...or worse, both.

"No, really, why would you say I'm a kindergarten teacher?" she persists, taking a step closer to me, and in this tiny space it feels almost intimate. Her breath wafts warm and sweet against my face, and I can just make out the soft scent of orange blossom from her hair. For a split second I have to stop myself from leaning forward and breathing her in.

"Is it just because I question your need to curse in front of a complete stranger even though there was no real reason to? That makes me a kindergarten teacher? Or is it because teachers are stuffy and dull and don't think that random cussing is 'cool'? Oh, forgive me, I just thought that meant you had manners and knew how to act appropriately in public, and if you accidentally touched a stranger's hand, you say sorry. Not vomit out some expletive and flap around like a pigeon with an injured wing!" Her voice grows louder and stronger with every word and she has me backed up against the shelf. She's almost a head shorter than me and as she's so close, I can see over the top of her head by just looking downward. The angle's giving me a pretty good view right down her shirt as well. And something between my legs likes what I'm seeing.

I throw up my hands in surrender and almost as a form of distraction.

"Whoa, whoa, whoa! Sorry, Mary. No... that's not why I asked if you were a kindergarten teacher. Though the lecture hardly disproves my theory," I add with a little snicker.

During my response, those intoxicating eyes have found mine again, and this time they're even rounder and wider than before. Sparkling with life, there's an internal light of their own that's dancing around in her velvet brown pupils. I swear I can see a hint of pink in her cheeks that wasn't there before her rant. Something makes me want to see how far I can make that blush spread down over her cheeks, down her neck, over her décolletage and-...I shake my head. Damn those eyes.

"Then what DID you mean?" She looks up at me, and for a moment she looks like she's really asking, and not just being combative. And there's something vulnerable in her voice that pushes me over the edge. Something that makes me wonder about the woman behind the nagging wench that's presenting itself to me now. Something that makes me want to really KNOW her, make her know me, trust me, open up to me.

"Well," I shrug as if there's a simple enough explanation, "I just meant...because I feel like laying down over your knee and letting you spank me."

Oh yeah, that should make her trust me.

Her mouth drops open. The action tears my eyes now down to her mouth. Her lips are soft and plump, dewy and pink like she's just taken a bite of a strawberry.

Except I have a feeling it's not the sweet juice of a berry that's about to come out from those lips.

"What the-..." she starts, then stops mid-sentence.

I grin at her, amused that the blush has actually progressed to a full-blown tomato rage red.

"Go on...say it..." I goad her.

"Say what?" She frowns.

"Say 'fuck,'" I lean on the word, almost sounding out each letter.

"I wasn't going to say...that." She purses her lips as her eyes follow suit and narrow at me.

"No, but you wanted to." I say, matter of factly.

She starts to protest, but I push on.

"You wanted to say... 'what the FUCK did you just say?' Go on, admit it! Admit that the cussing stranger made you want to cuss right back. At least have the guts to admit it." I cross my arms and lean back against the wall, grinning back at her.

She turns toward me, and now that we're standing a little further apart, it's not just individual features that have me staring at her, it's the whole damn package. She's petite and delectably curvy. Her mahogany brown hair is wavy and pulled into a messy bun, wisps falling to frame her face. She's dressed in a knee-length, black skirt and a blue pinstripe shirt. She should look plain but she's anything but. The material of her skirt finds every generous curve of her hips and thighs and her shirt's buttons struggle just a little to stay secure. Somehow, in the two minutes of standing here and sparring with her, I've made a definitive verdict about this woman - I want her.

"Hey. I wasn't going to say what you thought I was going to say." Her words drag my eyes back from roaming her body up to her face.

"No?" I can't focus on much more than sounding out one word as I try to regain control of my mind and body around this bewitching brunette.

"No." She looks quite defiant.

"Then what were you going to say, Mary?"

"Why are you calling me that?" She's distracted from the topic at hand by the nickname I have for her.

"Well, I don't know your name." I shrug.

"You could ask."

"Would you tell me?" I cock my eyebrow.

"Sure." It's her turn to shrug and I can't help but find the move adorable on her small frame.

"What is it?" I take the chance and ask.

"It's Mary," she tries to say with a straight face, but I notice the corners of her mouth twitch a little. She's thawing towards me. This I can work with.

"It is not," I contradict her. Almost out of habit now.

"What does it matter? You seem to know what I'm going to say before I say it anyway." She cocks her eyebrow now too. Mimicking me to mock me, and it's just making her all the more intriguing to me.

She does have a good point though, about me filling in the blanks even before she's said a word. The last few years I feel like I've been having the same conversation over and over again with women. But to be honest, it's been a long time since a woman has hated me on sight as I assume she does. It's refreshingly fun, almost. But I don't want her to hate me. Time to change tacks.

"Look, we got off to a bad start." I hold out my hand to her. "I'm Sebastian."

She takes a deep breath and looks at my outstretched hand as if wondering what to do with it. I have to bite the inside of my lip not to move my eyes down a few inches to watch the rise and fall of her chest.

"I'm... Cadence," she tells me, still ignoring my handshake offer though. Which is too bad, I'm craving a reason to touch her.

"Nice to meet you, Cadence. And what are you here for?" I cringe as I hear myself deliver that clichéd bar pick-up line.

"To pick up some cello rosin."

"Oh, me too, actually..."

We freeze, suddenly remembering what had brought us here in the first place.

And then we move, her reaching a hand out to push against my chest, but my arms are just that much longer and I grab the last tub of Pirazzi rosin from the shelf.

Her hand rests hot against me for a moment before she pulls it away. And I feel my body leaning forward, following her touch.

She looks up at me, with a pissed off look that has already become too familiar.

"I need that rosin, *Sebastian*." The sound of her voice speaking my name thrills me.

"Trust me, *Cadey*, I need it more." I speak her name hoping to provoke her into saying mine again.

"Don't call me that. It's Cadence. And it's not for me."

"Well, in that case, I get dibs, because it IS for me. Get a different brand. Or somewhere else." I'm not giving up.

"I can't, I have to buy it here. And…it's….it's for one of my students. He has his cello exam tomorrow," she says, resignedly.

"So, you ARE a teacher! I knew it!" I say gleefully, any win is sweet against this stubborn woman.

"Just give me the damn rosin!" she scoffs, stomping her foot in a way that makes her whole body shake, forcing me to stare her in the eye so I don't stare elsewhere.

"Aha! So, she DOES swear!" I hold my arms up in victory, garnering a look that almost wilts my manhood.

"'Damn' is not a swear word. It's just for emphasis. Like you're a 'damn' jerk!"

She tries to grab the rosin from my hand and the space between our fingertips cracks with electricity again. Her lips stretch against her teeth as she hisses and she wrenches her hand back and something in the sound makes my cock do what it's been threatening to do since I saw her. It grows instantly hard. Time to run.

"Fine. Then trust me when I want to emphasize this…it's been *damn* nice to meet you, *Mary*." I bend over and brush a soft kiss against her cheek. "And I promise I'll make it up to you," I say while waving the rosin at her, then turn and jog through the store before she can react.

"Pay the man, Jez!" I call out to my bandmate as I rush through the store's front door and into the waiting car, thinking of smelly garbage trucks and fermented Swedish fish to free the blood congregating in my groin.

But nothing can seem to fade the smell of orange blossoms against my lips.

Chapter Three

CADENCE

"And don't forget your Baroque period project due next Monday. Nothing except death will be accepted as an excuse for not turning it in. And even then, I want a death certificate signed by the state coroner. You've had all term, people."

With a wave of my hand I dismiss my last class to the sound of scraping chairs on the floor and chatter about everything but school work. I sink into my chair, exhausted, kicking my shoes off and rubbing one foot against the other.

The chaos of five hundred teenagers fleeing the confines of high school slowly dissipates and I let my body hang, completely lifeless in my desk chair, feeling the day seep slowly away from me.

But a part of it just won't budge.

Say 'fuck', I can still hear his voice taunt me. And the curve of his lip, goading me.

But it wasn't what he said but how he said it.

"Fuck." I turn the word over in my own mouth, remembering the way it sounded coming out of his. He made it sound like a proposition. One I'd have trouble refusing.

God, he was hot.

From the way his relaxed denim jeans had ridden low on his hips, showing his taut, ripped stomach when he reached up with his arms, to the red-tinted brown stubble on his strong chiseled jawline. From the infuriatingly long lashes that framed his jade green eyes, to the way his long fringe hung over his forehead, covering one eye. Even the small vertical scar that ran just across his top lip was provocative. Everything about him screamed sex. And it wasn't a scream I'd been receptive to recently.

But damn, he was a jerk. The cocky way he'd grinned when he made the comment about spanking him. I'd wanted to slap the arrogance right off his face.

Until he kissed you, that is, the annoying voice inside my head reminded me.

"He didn't kiss me," I argue back, out loud, while my cheek burned at the memory.

"Who didn't kiss you?" a female voice pipes up and I turn my head to the doorway.

"Ugh, nobody, an asshole at the music store," I tell my best friend and colleague, Sarah.

"But you wanted him to?" Her face lights up, always ready for a gossip, and always disappointed by my lack of ever having any.

"NO!" I yell, a little louder than I'd intended.

"WHOA!" I hear for the second time today. "So, someone you didn't want to kiss you…didn't kiss you." Sarah repeats, trying to make sense of something I don't have sense of yet.

"Right." I nod, hoping my apparent lack of information will stop her questions.

"So why are we talking about it?"

"We weren't."

"You were, alone here in your classroom," she points out.

"I was just…processing…"

"Right. So, um…what was this person like, who didn't kiss you, even though you didn't want him to?"

"He was…. infuriating!" I scrunch up my face again, remembering his face as he winked at me before he ran out of the store.

"And?"

"He STOLE from me!"

"He STOLE?" She looks even more confused than before.

"Well, kinda?" Well, he did, kind of.

"What did he steal?"

"My cello rosin!"

"How did he steal it? From your purse?"

"No, he just took it. In the store." Ugh, why isn't she getting it?

"So, he didn't pay??"

"No. Well, yes, his friend paid."

"He paid you?"

"No, he paid George, for the rosin."

"So, he stole from George?"

"No, I told you his friend paid." This was going nowhere.

"So, it ...wait. What? So, he didn't steal at all!"

"Yes! It was mine!"

"Had you paid for it?"

"No..."

"So..."

"Shut up, it was just mine, okay, and he took it. And then left." I cross my arms indicating I was done talking about this.

"Without kissing you." Ugh, again with the kissing. You'd think he'd kissed her.

"Yes. Well..." Technically...

"Wait. He DID kiss you?"

"Well, just on the cheek!"

"Way to bury the lead! Tell me about this cheek kisser!" Sarah jumps up at the word 'kisser' entirely too excited about nothing.

"I told you, he's a thief!" I frown at her. Whose side was she on?!

"You gotta let go of the rosin, babe," she sighs.

"Never! Anyway, I don't want to talk about it anymore." I wave my hand, dismissing any more questions.

"Fine. What are you doing tonight, other than not thinking about rosin-thieving cheek kissers?"

"Nothing. Which is exactly what I want to be doing, so whatever you're thinking, no."

"Come on, I have tickets to this amazing group called No Strings Attached, they're a string quartet playing mashups of classical music and rock covers."

"Wow. That sounds absolutely...horrendous." I shudder at what that might sound like.

"Why?"

"Er, hello. I'm a classically trained pianist and music teacher."

"Don't be such a snob. Trust me, they're brilliant. They just won a Grammy, first ever non-lyrical Brand New Artist winner! Anyway, you never go out anywhere with me. You know I have to live vicariously through you now that I'm married."

I did feel a little bad. I had been so busy with work lately that we'd hardly spent any time away from school together. She'd been there through everything good and bad in my life and I guess I could give her one night out.

"Fine. But I'm bringing a book," I warn her.

"YAY! Pick you up at 7:00." And she skips out of the room before I can change my mind.

Chapter Four

SEBASTIAN

"What time is it?" I get up from my seat for the fifth time in the last two minutes.

"Add about thirty-six seconds to what I told you the last time you asked." Brad answers from his spot on the beanbag, arms and legs spread out like an octopus, his violin bow see-sawing up and down, balancing on top of his forehead.

"I wasn't listening," I tell him honestly. I turn to the greenroom door and wrench it open, peering down the hallway at the crew rushing around, doing their jobs. Which includes ignoring me.

"Ask me again in thirty seconds," Brad offers.

"Gah, just fucking tell me already!" I slam the door shut and sit back down on the couch, pushing Jez's hand away when he puts in on my knee to stop the incessant jiggling.

"Chill, man, it's 6:30, we're on in an hour," Brad relents.

I don't think I can last an hour. My adrenaline has peaked and it needs to act now. My fingers are twitching, they've played the opening chord progressions of the first few songs over and over against my leg and they are itching to wrap around my cello.

"Can't we just go on now?" I ask my bandmates seriously, my leg jiggling so much the water in the jug on the coffee table builds up momentum and threatens to spill over the rim.

"No. Not if you want anyone to be there to listen, man." Jez answers, his voice trying to stay calm but ending up somewhere between amused and over it.

"Since when did we care if anyone was listening?" I'm getting desperate now. I stand back up and start to pace, drumming my fingers against my leg and biting the fingers on my left hand.

"Since we started charging them seventy dollars a pop to show up and listen." Marius calls out from his yoga stance in the corner. I feel like pushing him over and shoving his bow somewhere downward on his dog.

I can feel their eyes on me as I pace the room. Walking back and forth, corner to corner, around the chairs with no pattern in mind, muttering to myself, reminding myself of the set list, of opening and closing comments, crowd pleasers I can use.

"Man, he hasn't been this bad in a long time." I vaguely hear Marius say.

"Maybe since Amsterdam." Jez chuckles.

"Yeah?"

"Well, remember what happened in Amsterdam."

"No, I don't, dear Jeremy. Why don't you remind me?" Brad says to Jez, calling him by his full name.

"Why, Bradley, one might remember that one Mr. Sebastian had a visitor one night there in Amsterdam."

"Oh yes, one does remember. A rather loud visitor, if one does remember correctly."

"Oh yes, one does remember correctly indeed."

"It seems one's visitor helped wonders with Mr. Sebastian's preperformance jitters. Perhaps it is time we organized for Mr. Sebastian to have another visitor?"

"Isn't that Dennis' job?" Marius wonders

"It bloody hell isn't," says the voice booming through the intercom interrupting the banter.

"Aw fuck, who turned that on?" Jez growls at the baby monitor Dennis uses as an intercom to spy on us.

"Well, it wasn't me." Brad says defensively.

"No one's thinking it was you, Brad. When's the last time you turned anything on?" Marius quips, grinning at Jez and high fiving him.

"Hey!"

"I turned it on before you dickheads went in there." Dennis booms through the tiny speaker. "Now shut the fuck up and leave Sebastian alone. And Sebastian, stop fucking pacing, sit down and chill the fuck out. Remember the breathing lessons Hailey gave you."

I press myself against the door and close my eyes, counting my breaths. Deep breath in two, three, four, five. Hold. Out two, three, four, five. I feel my ribcage expand and stretch from the air. My hands feel the urge to scratch at my skin and I shove them in my pockets.

My right hand digs deep and closes around a cube object. It's the box of rosin. The rosin I stole from that woman. The woman in the store. Cadence. My mouth twitches a little as I remember the way her eyes rounded into large, perfect circles, the pupils like a Belgium chocolate truffle, soft brown and velvety, when I brushed her cheek with my lips. Her mouth shaped into a seductive 'O', in both sound and structure. Sending my body and mind into hormonal overdrive as I imagine her lips making that same shape while she experienced an 'O' of my making.

"Fuck." I shake my head to reset my brain's thoughts. What is wrong with me? Why has she taken such a hold of me?

"What?" Jez looks up in response to my curse.

"Nothing."

"He's thinking of a visitor."

I wasn't. But I am now. Thinking of opening the door to my dressing room and finding Cadence standing there. Even if just to yell at me for being a damn jerk again. I'd take it. I'd promised her I'd make it up to her. And I can't wait for the night to be over so I can fulfill that promise.

Just got. To get through. The night.

"Hey, what time is it now?" I ask the boys and they groan in synchrony.

"What?!?"

CADENCE

"You're not wearing that," Sarah greets me as soon as I open the door.

"What? Why? I think I look fine." I look down at my floor-length floral maxi dress and pink cardigan.

"You do, babe. You look fine. For church. Not a concert."

"A classical music concert!" I remind her.

"Mashed with ROCK!"

"Ugh, stop reminding me."

"Come on." She grabs my hand and pulls me into my bedroom.

"Where are we going?"

"Into the deepest corners of your closet to find something appropriate for you to wear."

***

"I look ridiculous," I tell her ten minutes later sitting in her car. My floral dress has been discarded and in its place is a short black mini I bought on a whim once but have never had the courage to wear. After some begging, Sarah finally relented and allowed me to pull on the pink cardigan.

"Only because you keep fidgeting." She reaches over and slaps my hands away from my cardigan's collar.

"We're going to stand right out." I scrunch my face up at the thought.

"So, what if we do?" She shrugs nonchalantly. "But trust me, we're going to fit right it."

"You're crazy. We're going to be the only ones dressed like this."

She turns into the parking lot and waits for the crowd of people crossing to get to the concert hall. A startling array of leather and Mohawks and motorcycle boots greet me.

"Oh. Never mind," I concede.

Sarah throws her head back and laughs, "I told you."

"Curiouser and curiouser."

She parks the car and we get out. I pull on the dress, making sure it covers top and bottom where it needs to. It does, just barely. The pink cardigan covers my arms but just barely buttons up over my chest, so I leave it open.

"Come on!" Sarah calls out to me, waving at me to catch up with her. "Let's go see Beethoven roll over in his grave!"

***

"Aren't these seats amazing?" Sarah squeals to me, turning in her seat to take in the sold-out crowd.

Despite myself, I have to agree with her. Somehow, she's scored front row seats and the atmosphere is electric. I have to admit, I have no idea what to expect, but I'm a little excited. As a lifelong lover of classical music this concept of mashing it with rock music sounds almost sacrilegious. The crowd is an eclectic mix at best – and there is an unprecedented number of young women here, more than I've ever seen at a classical music performance.

The stage setup tells me nothing. There isn't any decor, just an empty stage with four chairs. Not even a music stand disrupts the otherwise bare landscape of the stage floor.

Who are these musicians?

With the building noise from the rowdy crowd, my curiosity grows, and by the time the lights dim and the 10,000 voices around me start chanting "No Strings Attached! No Strings Attached!" I find my lips twitching to join them. Nothing stops Sarah though, and she's up and out of her chair, pumping her fists and adding her yells with the crowd's as the hall completely fades into black.

I hold my breath as my eyes adjust to the darkness.

Then a single note plays pure and clear, fading in from the dark to fill the hall with sound. I close my eyes and feel the vibration of the cello string penetrate my body. My cells calibrate to the particular vibration of that one cello. And I wait.

The single note breaks and it's silent again.

Then, as if ordained by God, the ceiling of the concert hall lights up with 100,000 white lights. Twinkling artificial stars dancing over the eaves and chandeliers, reflecting back onto the darkened walls and raised hands of the audience, reaching out to touch the radiance. As each light grows brighter, and its diameter spreads so you can't differentiate one from the next, the single string note plays once more, starting soft and then building louder and louder and louder as the light grows brighter and brighter until the ceiling is just one giant expanse of light, almost painfully blinding, bathing the entire audience in an almost heavenly pure glow. Just when I think the light can't get brighter, it explodes like a hundred fireworks and then folds into darkness once more.

And then the music begins. Out of the darkness, while my eyes are still playing tricks on me and projecting dancing fairy lights against the black backdrop, the single note breaks into the opening strains of a tune so familiar, but I can't pick it.

I don't care. It is divine.

Short notes on the violins dance over the driving beat of the cellos. I'm lost in the sound, with the lights completely out, my senses are all forced to shut down to focus only on the music coming out of the dark.

The notes cascade over each other, driving forward, forward, building towards a chorus that I can feel is about to break.

God, what is that tune...what is it?

I reach out next to me and Sarah's hand gropes for mine, and we grip each other for a sense of reality in this surreal, beautiful experience. Her body bumps against mine as we give in to the sound wrapping itself around us.

And then, as the chords change in a familiar progression, I realize, it's U2's "It's a Beautiful Day".

I'm stunned. I've only ever heard the lyrical version; I am amazed at the melodic beauty of this song now that I don't have the words to focus on. It's almost as if this piece of music was written to be played by these four string musicians, they've made it their own.

But I don't have time to muse over my revelation for too long.

Just as the chorus breaks, and the crowd raises their voices into a communal declaration of "It's a Beautiful Day", the stage lights up with a universe of dancing stars as if fallen from the ceiling.

The scream that projects from the crowd somehow is only just overtaken by the music, and I scan the stage, trying to make out the band amongst the white haze.

As the song descends into the second verse, the lights slowly dissipate, and focus on a single spotlight, on the lead cellist.

As my eyes blink away the excessive light, I start to see the musician's form. It's tall and slim, his head is down, hair over his face as he stands, lost in the music he is creating from his instrument. Or is it that it is creating the music from him? It's hard to tell, they look to be working in complete synchrony. In all my years of attending both classical and pop concerts, I've never experienced anything like it.

I can't tear my eyes off the cellist, envious of his talent, of his connection to the music, maybe even jealous of his commitment to the notes, his complete surrender to his passion.

And then, just as the song builds to its climax, he throws his head back, the hair falling from his eyes and he looks out

into the crowd. And my blood runs cold even as my body bursts into flame.

It's him.

And my blood runs cold even as my body bursts into flame.

It's him.

Chapter Five

SEBASTIAN

I don't know if it's my breath, or Jez's next to me, that is hissing in my ears. But it's definitely my own blood I can hear coursing through my veins. It's amazing that I can hear anything over the crowd but it's right there, in my ears, racing too fast to use to keep time. The ceiling light show is fading and we've just run on stage with whatever light there is left. Once it's completely dark, I count under my breath - one, two, three, four and pull my bow.

That first note is always the hardest.

The sound to break the tension, to build the excitement, to meet and raise the expectation.

While we take turns taking the lead during our performances, that wuss ass Jez will never play that first note. So, no wonder it's me pacing the greenroom before every show.

But here. Now. I'm glad that mofo doesn't get to do this.

I wouldn't give anything up for the feeling this gives me.

Knowing that it's *that* sound, the whisper from *my* bow against the cello string, singing out to this crowd, who have paid, can you believe, it? PAID! To come here and listen to us, is from *me*.

Yeah, I brought you here. And I'm going to give you the show of your life. I make my promise to the crowd.

I break the monotony of the single note once I know I have the crowd's attention, and break into the intro to U2's "It's a Beautiful Day".

Every time I play this, I remember the day we picked it. It was after our first paid gig in a tiny pub in Edinburgh and after a long night drinking away our pitiful pay, we stepped out onto the empty streets feeling on top of the world. We ran all the way back to our backpacker's motel singing "it's a beautiful day!" at the top of our lungs and in our rehearsal the very next day, we arranged it into our now trademark opening.

I hear Jez and then Brad and then Marius' instruments join mine in turn, and for a moment, I can't help but grin at how we, the idiot boys of our class, can make such beautiful music, and even more unbelievably, do it together.

Jez's cello's notes dance around mine, our instruments whispering and yelling at one another in kind, like lovers in the most tumultuous and passionate relationship. We know each other's parts so well, we could chop and change between us without a beat. Something Dennis made us promise to stop doing just to try to trip the other up.

But today, today I'm lost in my own performance. It's been a while since we've been on stage, and I've missed it. I close my eyes and just let my fingers do their thing. I've learned long ago never to interfere too much, my body knows what and how to play better than I could ever consciously tell it to. I feel the sweat start to drip from my forehead onto the flop of fringe covering my eyes.

The second verse comes before I know it, and the lights start to fade in, focusing on me. This is usually the first time I can get a really good look at the audience. I flip my head back, and with a puff of air, blow the hair out of my eyes. I look out into the crowd. It's a sold-out performance. I skim the tops of heads and moving bodies. Until my eye catches on someone in the front row. She's not moving. She's standing still amongst the sea of writhing bodies. And her eyes are closed, her hands clasped like in prayer, her lips resting on the tips of her touching index fingers. She's mesmerizing to me. A figure of peace amongst total anarchy.

And then the world comes falling down.

She opens her eyes and it's her.

The girl with the perfect moon eyes.

Cadence.

***

"What the hell happened in our intro man?" Jez pushes the door open to the restroom and confronts me.

As soon as we'd left the stage for intermission, I'd run off to the little boy's room to go relieve myself. Also, in part because I knew this confrontation was coming.

"What do you mean?" I know exactly what he meant. But there was no way in the world I was going to be telling him.

"You missed a whole fucking section!" He throws his arms up in the air in frustration.

"It wasn't any big deal, mate, you took over."

"Yeah, but give me a head's up next time." He calms down, but is still frowning.

"What's with the hard time, mate? We used to switch it up all the time." *Yeah, that's right,* I tell myself, *deflect, Jez just loves when I do that.*

"Don't fucking make it about me, Seb. Something happened and it freaked you out, and I want to know what."

"It wasn't anything! Get off my case, geez. I've covered for you a hundred times," I say before I can stop myself.

Jez stops and grabs my arm. "Hey. I'm just trying to make sure you're okay, you don't have to-...you know."

I instantly feel bad and grab his hand still wrapped around my arm and squeeze. "I'm sorry, Jez. Fuck. It's...I just saw a woma- person, I knew."

His face relaxes and a cheeky grin starts to spread across his mouth. Ugh. I should've just let him continue to worry.

"Ohhh, a 'woma-person'? I see. And does this 'woma-person' have a name? Or do we just know her by her measurements?" He sounds just about as gleeful as I've ever heard him, opening the restroom door and letting me out.

"Oh, fuck off!" I shove him on the shoulder and take off down the hallway to my dressing room. I can hear his footsteps running behind me to catch up and I storm ahead, barreling through the door and pushing it closed behind me, locking it fast. I hear him slam against the locked door and curse.

"Fuck! Bastard! Let me in!"

I ignore him and collapse on the couch, flipping the switch on the light, bathing the room in total darkness. I'm craving just a moment to myself. Myself and my thoughts. I try to zone out the banging on the door, covering my head with a cushion.

The darkness allows the questions in my head to focus.

Focus on her.

She was the reason I'd missed the beat and Jez had had to jump in and take over the lead. She was the last person I'd expected to see in the crowd, it's almost as if I'd conjured her into being just from thinking of her all afternoon.

What is she doing here?

Well, duh. She came to see the band. Then why didn't she recognize me from the music store? Did I look that different in person? Good different? Or bad different?

She, on the other hand, didn't look any different. Fuck, she looked so good. There in her mismatched outfit. Short, barely there black mini dress and the woolen pink cardi. She looked sweet and so fucking sexy at the same time. I didn't know whether I wanted to take her home to meet my parents, or drag her backstage and make myself blissfully acquainted with every single inch of her body.

God, the way she looked up at me with those perfectly round eyes of hers. At one point she looked as surprised to see me as I did her.

I'd recovered after the intro, and spent the last forty-five minutes see-sawing between staring at her and trying to not look at her at the same time. She was obviously trying to do the same as I'd either catch her looking at me and she'd look away immediately or she'd turn back to me and I'd be the one to look away.

But I couldn't look away for long.

I'd wanted to know what my music was doing to her.

And I'd wanted her to know that tonight, I was playing for her.

CADENCE

"Wowwwwww," Sarah lets out a long, satisfied sigh, and I'm almost inclined to ask her if she wants a cigarette. "That was amazing." She leans back against her chair as everyone around us shuffles out to get a drink or stretch their legs during the intermission.

I don't say anything.

I can't.

Because 'amazing' and 'wow' just don't cut it.

Calling it 'classical mashed with rock' is just about the biggest injustice I've heard in a long time. They'd taken iconic modern rock and pop songs, and classical pieces hundreds of years old and completely made them their own. After the epic opening, they'd pulled back on the pace and played a somber and haunting version of the Gladiator Movie theme interspersed with the cello part of Autumn from Vivaldi's "Four Seasons". The interweaving of the two pieces was seamless as if they'd been made to be played as one.

And then one after another, the songs had come, surprising in their range and variety. But there had been no bigger surprise than the sheer talent of the band.

And one member in particular.

I hadn't been able to take my eyes off Sebastian during the whole set. From that first moment we locked eyes during "It's A Beautiful Day", this concert became something different than any other concert I have been to, it felt like it was a concert for me. There is no reason for it other than, I guess, having had the interaction with a member of the band just hours earlier. But something, something unexplainable made me feel like...it was for me.

"Come on, I need to go use to ladies." I stand up and grab Sarah's arm, who protests. "Oh hush, I'll buy you a poster or something."

"Oh, YAY! I can kiss it good night." She springs to her feet, gathering her things. "Did you see how freakin' hot they all were?"

"Um, no." I hadn't. I'd just noticed the one.

***

"Where is the bloody thing?" We open a door and step out into the darkness.

"I don't know, that guy just pointed out here," Sarah says, suddenly clinging to my arm a little too tightly.

"Well, it looks like a death alley." There's a sliver of light about fifty feet away and I consider running to it instead of just walking.

"I'll protect you with my rolled-up poster," Sarah promises to defend me, even as she hides behind me.

"Yeah, thanks. Ok, look, if it's not around the corner, we'll just go back," I say, wondering where my bravado is coming from.

We suddenly hear footsteps behind us and we start walking faster.

"Hey!" a voice calls out to us.
"Fuck! Should we run?" Sarah whispers to me.
"Hey, are you girls okay?" another voice speaks up.
And I freeze and turn back towards it.
"Hi, Cadence."

Chapter Six

SEBASTIAN

Her friend replies before she does.

"Wow. You guys are with...you're the band."

Jez grins that grin of his I've seen him lure thousands of women with, and reaches out his hand, "And you are?"

But she seems to know just the kind of smile Jez has given her, "I am... married," she replies, matching his grin, but just for a moment, before she turns to Cadence. "Wait. He called you by your name. Do you two know each other? You told me you'd never heard of them before."

I watch her, dying to know the answer myself.

Cadence looks up at me, her eyes locking with mine. I blame the sudden racing of my heart on the short run Jez and I had just taken to catch up to the women. I cock an eyebrow, waiting for her answer, but she seems tongue tied.

"Um, no. We, er, we just met briefly today," I speak up, just to break the silence.

"Today?" Her friend frowns a little, as if turning something over in her brain. "When did you meet anyone today? You were at work all day, until lunch time when you went to..." Suddenly, everyone turns to me. "You're the bloody rosin thief!"

Cadence's mouth drops open and her eyes grow wide. She grabs her friend's arm and shushes her. "Shut up, Sarah!"

Sarah just shrugs her off and turns back to me, her face excited. I wonder what I'm in for. "You are, aren't you? The one who took the last rosin she needed for class. She's been going on about that rosin all day. She didn't mention how good-looking you are, though...or that you're a freakin' celebrity!"

I cover my face with my hand, unable to hide the smile at the news that I've been on her mind as much as she's been on mine.

"Yeah. You really pissed her off," her friend adds.

Oh. Okay, maybe not for the same reason though.

Cadence groans and the sound is seductive. I'm finding it hard not to try to commit every look, every sound of hers to memory.

"I promised you I'd make it up to you," I say to Cadence, feeling like it's a promise for so much more than pilfered rosin.

"That's *only* if I give you the chance," she finally speaks up. The challenge sends a chill through me. It's been a while since a woman spoke to me this way.

Most of the time they're falling over themselves to tell me how much they love me.

Jez guffaws next to me and I guess he's figured out who the reason was for my slip-up during our intro. Which means he's enjoying her challenge to me a little too much.

"And why wouldn't you?" I ask her, and hold my breath for the answer.

She looks at me, and I can see something in the back of her eyes, playful but dangerous. Who is this woman?

"Well, what chance does a thief have to make it up to me when I still owe him a spanking?" She shrugs a little to make her point and stares me down.

"Whooooaaa," Sarah and Jez exclaim simultaneously, and Jez hops up and down a little out of pure excitement. I want to kick him in the shin, but I'll save it for later when I'm not being scrutinized by this strange creature.

"Be honest, Mary, you kinda want to give me that spanking now, don't you?" I grin at the way she cringes on hearing my nickname for her, but I can tell she won't give into the urge to ask me about it.

"Only to teach you the lesson in politeness that you've obviously need," she counters.

"Ooooh!" Our two spectators gasp.

"I'm plenty polite. In fact, I remember I thanked you with a kiss," I say, pressing my finger to my temple as if in thought.

"What?" Jez yells out.

"Oh relax, it was just a kiss on the cheek," Sarah tells him. And I flush at the knowledge that she shared that news with her friend as well.

"I'm not surprised that you think that an unrequited and unwanted kiss is polite," Cadence comments.

"Was it?" I ask, taking a step closer to her and lowering my voice, the mood suddenly changing.

"Was it what?" She tries to back away but I follow her.

"Unwanted?" I whisper by her ear. The return of that orange blossom scent is making me dizzy.

The pause is felt by everyone and is only broken when the bell signaling the end of intermission rings.

"Fuck!" Jez grabs my hand and pulls me back to the door, "We're gonna be fucking late!"

I wave him off and he shakes his head and runs off, leaving me behind.

I need my answer.

"Cadence? Was it unwanted?" I press her for an answer.

I want to reach out for her, the uncertainty making me feel weak. I want to touch her, to know that she and what I'm feeling are real.

The back of my hand skims her cheek. It's warm. She says nothing.

"Cadence. We better go," Sarah speaks up, forgotten by both of us.

The bell dings again and I can't ignore it.

I tear myself away and run down the alley, and just as I wrench the door open to run inside, I think I hear a whisper.

A whisper that tells me, "No, no, it wasn't."

CADENCE

"What. The Fuck. Just Happened?" Sarah asks me when we're back in our seats waiting for the second set to start.

"I don't...I don't know."

"What happened between you two at the store?" she presses on.

"Nothing."

"Come on, the way you two were talking and touching...it can't have been nothing."

"I'm telling you, it was nothing. We were there for about two minutes, and then he stole the rosin, kissed my cheek and ran off."

"You seemed like...like...old lovers or something."

"Oh, shush." I brush away her words.

"Honey..." She touches my arm and I turn to face her. "I'm serious. He has it bad for you. And, you've definitely got...something for him," she says, choosing her words carefully.

"Yeah. In the eight years you've known me...have I ever given you any reason to think of me as a person who would have it bad for someone?"

"No. Until just then," she says pointedly.

The lights go down and I'm glad. I can't keep the act up for long, and I can't process my thoughts without her haranguing me for answers I don't have, and don't want to share with anyone.

The second act starts like the first one, in complete darkness. It gives the audience no choice but to focus on the music. The music that deserves our complete and undivided attention.

The clearest note rings out, that one single note, enveloping my consciousness, building and building the anticipation, until I realize I haven't taken a breath in so long. The mind races, trying to generate a melody from the one note, craving for a resolution to the question – what song are they going to play next?

And then, the stage explodes into light, and the opening strains to Ram Jam's "Black Betty" blasts from the speakers. Four spotlights focus on the band, all four on their feet, facing each other in the middle of the stage, completely engrossed in their own instruments, but creating a sound that carries as one. Sarah and I can't help but jump to our feet along with the 10,000 people around us, the crowd singing along to the music.

My eyes are cemented to Sebastian. His hands dancing over the cello, like he was born to create this music. His utter commitment to the performance taking a hold of my own music-obsessed mind and I can't help but wonder what it would be like to be with someone who so intrinsically understood that passion of mine.

My hand comes up to touch my cheek, the spot he's touched twice now. It burns hot, as if the blood in my whole body has rushed to that spot to make a connection with him.

I can't remember when I've ever felt so alive.

I know why I can't remember.

Because I've never ever felt this way.

***

"You guys have been fucking amazing! The best in the world!!! We are so bloody down with down under!!" the other cellist, Jez, shouts into the microphone as the boys take their bow.

We're all on our feet. Bodies sweaty from dancing, spirits full and satisfied from the musical feast we've had. I wring my hands to stop them from reaching out to Sebastian as he moves off the stage, his eyes locking with mine for a moment, a soft smile playing on his lips.

I can't help but wonder if this is the last time I'll ever see him. And the idea fills me with a terror that is disproportionate to the time I've known him. Which only makes me more afraid.

The stage is empty and the chorus starts to build. "Encore, encore, encore!" Sarah shouts at the top of her lungs along with the crowd.

I hold my breath.

Anything for more.

The yells and claps start even before I notice him come on stage.

He's alone.

His cello in one hand he walks to the microphone.

"This is for someone. She knows who she is."

I vaguely feel a pain in my arm that I guess is Sarah digging her nails into my biceps.

But I don't care. He's moved his chair right up to the edge of the stage and in front of my seat.

He runs his hand through his sweaty fringe, pushing it back from his forehead and he stares at me for a second before closing his eyes, and pulls his bow across the strings.

I don't know what I expect but it wasn't this.

Within seconds, I and the entire audience double over in laughter as the song emanating from his cello is the one and only Carly Jae Jepsen classic "Call Me Maybe".

I look up at him through laughter-induced tears and he has the most camp look on his face as he sings along with the crowd "Hey, I just met you, and this is crazy, but here's my number, so call me maybe." At one point he stops playing and mimes the phone up against his ear, using the old rotary dialing telephone and the audience erupts into even louder hysteria.

And then, without missing a step, he puts the imaginary phone down and starts to play again, this time, it's The Police's "Every Breath You Take".

The way he plays it, it sounds like it was made to be a cello solo. It's haunting and beautiful, soulful and somber. It's perfection.

I feel my hands clasp each other and rest against my chin as I watch him. Drinking in everything about him, his movements, his facial expressions, his breaths.

I don't want it to end.

But it does.

And the applause is louder than anything we've heard that night.

He stands and winks to me, pulls something from his pocket and throws it to me.

It's the cello rosin box. I open it and take the jar of amber balm out and see it's wrapped in a piece of paper. I unfold the paper and mouth the words written there, "See me backstage, maybe?"

I look up at the stage and he's gone.

I guess he made it up to me after all.

Chapter Seven

SEBASTIAN

I run off the stage to the sound of the applause so loud I can't even hear my footsteps stomping on the metal staircase leading down to the backstage.

The sights around me are a blur, my heart's beating so fast I'm trying to take deep breaths to stop it from thumping right out of my chest. The combination of ending the show, and the performance for Cadence have me reeling. The head rush is better than the drugs we used to think we were so cool for trying.

A hard thump on my back stops me on my way to the backstage door where I'm hoping she'll be waiting for me.

"Ma-ate!" Dennis grins at me. It's really the only time he's ever really happy, when a show's gone well and he can relax for five minutes before the next one. "That was phenomenal."

I grin back at him, his happy face a welcome sight compared to the sourpuss he can be when we're on tour. "Thanks, man."

"That thing with the girl...gold. Why didn't you tell me you were going to do that? I woulda made sure we had some cameras on you."

"Um, it was just spur of the moment." Except that I'd always planned to do it...for the right person.

"Great, great...you seemed so romantic even I wanted to give you a big ol' kiss on the mouth."

I wrap him up in a big hug. For all the stress he gives us, I know he's all heart when it comes to us and the band. Then I kiss him on the cheek and he pushes me away with a big growl!

"Hey! None of that...we gotta keep up the image that you're a single lothario!"

"Oh, no, Dennis, everyone knows I've only got eyes for you!" We laugh and grab each other in a hug again, the high from the show still streaming through our veins.

"Come on, everyone's waiting for you in the greenroom." He pulls on my arm.

Not everyone, I think to myself. But I know he won't take no for an answer. I figure I'll make an appearance and then slip out. It should take her a few minutes to get backstage anyway.

"Lead the way, Big D!"

We race to the greenroom and yank the door open.

The usual sight greets us. Something between a high school party and a low rate opium den in Amsterdam. Young, pretty girls crammed into every inch, the lights are off, only the glow from the TV illuminates the sweaty bodies in the room.

"SEBASTIAN! SEBASTIAN! SEBASTIAN!" The boys raise their voices in a chant and the twenty other people crammed into the tiny smoke-filled room follow along.

"Yes, boys, I am Sebastian," I play along when the chant dies down. "Your God hath arrived, and your wish is my command!"

A paper cup thwacks me on the side of the head. "We wish for more ice!" Marius yells out from under a pile of arms and legs and blonde hair.

A loud cheer erupts and I notice Jez in the corner with each of his arms wrapped around a girl's shoulders. He grins at me and whispers something to one of them before getting up and following me out to the hallway.

"Hey, you all right?" he asks me.

I nod, "I guess I don't have to ask how you're doing?"

He shrugs and gives me a lopsided smile, "Can't complain. These Australian girls are wild. Can we move here?"

"You say that now, but two weeks from now I look out the window and you'll be hanging onto the wing of the first Qantas flight out of here."

"There's a beauty in there, Mandy. Fits right in with the Sebastian type. Want me to introduce you?"

"Nah, mate, I'm...a, I'm a little tired. Not used to the long shows yet."

He peers at me a little worried. "You sure you're okay? It's not that girl, Cadence, right? That's just you having a bit of fun?"

"Yeah, yeah. No, seriously, just gonna have a quick nightcap and head back to the hotel, I think." Hopefully not alone, I don't add.

"Ok, man, take it easy. I'm gonna..." he gestures with his head back to the room.

"Go back to work?"

"It's a hard job, mate." He grins and punches me on the shoulder lightly before slipping back into the room.

I put the ice bucket down and catch my reflection in one of the mirror doors.

I'm a mess. Sweat dripping from every pore, my hair doing some sort of bird nest impersonation, my shirt drenched.

"Not sexy." I say to my mirror image.

I check my watch; I should have enough time to quickly change into another shirt. On my way to my dressing room, I pass Mark, our head of security.

"Mark! I'm just getting refreshed in my dressing room. If a girl comes looking for me, just send her there, okay?!"

He grins and I roll my eyes at him. Our security team is used to our playboy ways on the road by now, but it's been a while since I had someone come to my dressing room compared to the other guys, so he's obviously getting a little bit more of a kick out of it than usual.

I rip the shirt off me even before I get to the door. Pulling the leather pants off my legs, I kick them into the corner and jump around a bit to air dry the sweat clinging to my skin.

There's a knock on the door.

Fuck, that was quick. The butterflies in my stomach are both surprising and refreshing. And I try not to focus on them as I pull on a pair of jeans and a t-shirt.

"Just a sec! I'm just getting decent!"

I run my hands through my hair as I get to the door and pull it open.

"Hey," she says.

And for a moment, my mind goes completely blank.

CADENCE

"OMG!" Sarah squeals in my ear reading the note from Sebastian over my shoulder. "What are you going to do?"

I glare at her to scare her into lowering her voice. I'm already getting enough daggers and curious looks from the audience around me as the lights go up and everyone gets up to leave.

I sink down into my chair, blankly watching everyone else crowd into the aisles, emptying the hall.

What am I going to do? That's a good question.

Is it? I ask myself again.

When have I ever thought that going backstage to meet some rockstar like a seventeen-year-old groupie was a good idea? Well, maybe when I was a seventeen-year-old groupie, but life has knocked that desire right out of me and it's been a long time since I'd been interested in any man let alone one that was 100% bound to break my heart.

"Dude. You're not actually considering not going?" Sarah looks at me in horror. I can only imagine how the concept would horrify her romantic sensibilities. She watches dog weddings on YouTube and cries, for god's sake.

But Sarah and I are a world apart. She married her high school sweetheart and I have more baggage than the luggage carousel at Sydney International Airport. And until today, I hadn't had any problems sticking with my vow to avoid any and all relationships if possible. Until today, that is, until something, some*one*, came along and made the risk almost worth it. Almost.

"Sare, seriously. What do we think's going to happen here? At most we have some short fling while he's in Oz and a week from now I'm waving forlornly with my face pressed against the window as his private plane flies away and by the next news cycle I see him going to some awards show with a Kardashian?" I ask her, airing my worst fears.

"Whoa. How long have you been thinking about this?"

"Too long!!" I admit to her.

She sighs and sits down next to me, pulling on my arm and making me face her.

"Honey. Did you have a good time tonight?"

I look her in the eye and I can't lie. "Yes," I tell her, because I did. I'd loved it. Everything. I'd loved everything about the evening. The going out, the spending time with my friend, the music, the attention from the sexy, crazy talented man.

"And would you have had fun tonight if I hadn't made you come out?" She presses.

I scrunch my face up, because we both know the answer. "No."

"And ... do you like him?"

She knows she doesn't have to ask the question. Just as I know I don't need to answer it. We both know I haven't had this kind of connection with a man in a long time.

"So, just trust me, you need this. Don't I know you better than anyone?" she dares me to challenge her. The list of people who really know me at all is short, but she really is at the top of it, so I just nod.

"So, take a chance! If it all goes to shit, I'll be the first one over with a tub of hazelnut ice cream and a spoon."

I take a deep breath. She's right. I've been in hibernation, in hiding too long. I never wanted to be this person, this person who was afraid to live. I had to leave the past behind.

"Ahhhh! Let's go!" I leap out of the seat, clutching the rosin box and note in my hand.

"Woohooo!" she yells with excitement and follows me to the backstage door.

***

"Yeah, just turn the corner and it's the third door on your left," the giant wall of man labeled 'Mark' tells me, before winking and adding, "It's a popular destination tonight."

I frown and glance at Sarah. She just shrugs and pushes gently on my back.

"Come on, babe. What do you expect, he's an important guy around here?"

That's exactly what I was afraid of.

"Wait." Sarah grips my arm to stop me for a moment. She runs her fingers through my hair fluffing it up a little.

"Thanks, MOM!" I stick my tongue out at her playfully, secretly glad she is here. I wouldn't be brave enough to do this on my own.

"Not done yet," she cups the underside of my breasts and bounces them up a bit.

"Hey!" I push her hands away and she pouts.

"Just helping!"

"Yeah, helping yourself, more like!"

She grins, not denying it. "You look beautiful. But he already knows that. What he might not know is how unpunctual you are. Come on!"

We turn the corner and come to a screaming halt.

He's standing at his doorway, his body wrapped around a stunning, tall, blonde woman.

We watch as they pull apart, gazing at one another, unable to take their eyes off the other person. The look seems to last forever, and then they pull each other into a long tight hug again, and then he pulls her into his room to the sound of her soft laughter and shuts the door.

I can hear Sarah holding her breath next to me.

"Don't say it," I softly beg her.

"Say what?" she asks softly.

"Say, I should go up there anyway."

"Ok. I wasn't going to."

"Just give me a minute."

"Ok."

I take a breath and will myself to walk to his door. Each step is harder than the last but it's only ten more and I count them in my head. I stand outside for a second, staring at his name printed on the sheet stuck on the door, wondering how my life might've been different, if I'd been the one on the other side of the door, and it saddens me more than I expect. I crouch down and leave the box of rosin and the note on the floor and walk back to my friend and out of Sebastian's life.

Chapter Eight

CADENCE

The school orchestra erupts into their finale.

One, two, three, four, my baton keeps the time while I gesture to the brass section to keep their build on the crescendo...hold it...hold it...my hand directs them...and go!

They break into an almost chaotic burst of sound. Almost. But these kids aren't the best in this school for nothing. Controlled but fierce. They bring the epic piece to a breathtaking halt.

We all hold our breaths as the sounds fade.

Then Greyson, the first flute, jumps up and says what we're all thinking, "Yeehaw, we all finished at the same time!"

I can't help but join them in their laughter. But my heart weighs a little heavy with the news I'm about to have to give them.

"Great job, everyone. That was probably our best run-through yet!" I smile at them, just wanting to give them a moment to enjoy the progress they've made in the last two months. Putting in the extra rehearsals and even one-on-one time with me to perfect their individual parts and solos. "Kids, before you go, there's just some news."

The noise from their packing up stops. They know me pretty well and I guess they can hear the apprehension in my voice.

"As you know, the band trip to the Nationals is going to cost a lot. We've applied for our full orchestra which is almost fifty of you. So, that's, well, it's a lot."

"Miss Bray..."

"Just a sec, Greyson. The school isn't normally budgeted for the trip, mostly since this is the first time we've made it to Nationals for a long time. So, look, we're trying to get the money, it's just not a given yet."

"How bad is it, Miss Bray?"

"Honestly, at this point, I'm not going to lie to you, it's not looking great. But I don't want you to give up. I promise you guys, I'm going to do whatever it takes, okay? We haven't worked so hard for nothing! okay, guys?"

I get a small murmur in response.

"Come on, guys, you can do better than that. You with me, guys?"

"YES, MISS BRAY!"

"That's better. So, kids, get outta here and don't think we're not having an extra rehearsal this weekend."

I give each of the kids a smile as they march out, instruments and bags in hand. I can tell my news is weighing heavily on them. Five years ago, the school didn't even have a music program. After I came here as a substitute teacher and heard how some of the kids wanted to learn the piano, I started to teach them in groups after school.

Slowly more and more kids came out of the woodwork. Some with no music training at all, some whose parents were driving an hour out of the way for practical and theory classes because the school wasn't providing them.

Together with Sarah, who was also new at the school, we applied and were granted a small music budget for the school. And the more the music program grew, the more students were wanting to join and learn. Too many than the small grants could stretch to. But I didn't have the heart to say no to them. How do you say no to a child who is begging you to learn something that you can teach them? But the school could barely afford new resources for the library and computer labs, and as too often is the case, music and art are viewed as luxuries.

So, the last five years have been scrimping and saving. The music program students and I on the weekends, out washing cars and selling chocolates. Buying hand-me-down instruments at yard sales and barely readable orchestral scores. But those things didn't matter to me, and it didn't matter to the kids. All that mattered was we could get together and make music.

Five years ago, there was nothing and now the school's orchestra has beaten every other school in their region and earned their spot in the Nationals. The only thing that was going to stop that bus leaving for Canberra was my dead body.

I walk around the music room, tucking in the chairs and putting away the music stands. I run my fingers over the old baby grand piano left to us by a benefactor in his will who had a grandchild who attended the school. I sit down and wiggle around on the stool, enjoying the squeaks and creaks it makes as I get comfortable.

My fingers graze the keys.

I love the sound of this old piano. The hours I've spent hearing new students fumble and find their way around it, and the sheer perfection that is the performance of some of the more advanced students. Making classics by Beethoven and Mozart their own.

I play the beginning notes of Beethoven's "Fur Elise" and hum along.

"Dum dum dum dum dum ...dum da da da..."

I close my eyes, letting my fingers find their own way over the keys. After "Moonlight Sonata", it's probably one of the most popular piano pieces in history and the bane of every piano teacher's existence.

But I love it.

The simplicity, the pure classical form of question and answer. I wonder if there's been a single day since I learned the piece myself when I haven't played it. I know this piece like most people know how to breathe. It just comes naturally from somewhere within me. An involuntary action that comes from somewhere in the very genetics of your body, your cells.

The music coming from my fingers lifts my spirit and I feel it start to erase the stress and worry of the day away.

"Da dum dum da... da da da dumm."

I think I'm smiling as I hum along which would probably look silly to someone who couldn't feel what I'm feeling, as the music permeates my body and mind.

My fingers can feel the ending is coming and I have to hold them back to stop them from rushing to the end and let it come as Beethoven intended. In the notes' own pace and time.

I giggle a little. And then giggle at my giggle. I shouldn't be so happy at playing such a common, simple piece. But to me that's the best music of all.

A clap from the doorway startles me and I can see a reflection in the piano's polished woodwork even before I turn.

He's back.

SEBASTIAN

I watch the kids stream out of the school's double doors. There are more than I imagined could be crammed into what looks like an average-sized school building.

While I wait for the school to empty, I count the windows and wonder which one is Cadence's classroom. And if she's there looking out at me.

I can't believe I'm here. Like some creepy stalker, scouring the Australian coast looking for a woman I met in a store for two minutes once. Put like that, it really does make me sound crazy. But the crazy part is that it doesn't feel wrong at all.

Why I've felt like I can't take a full breath unless I'm in her presence since the moment we met, I don't know. Why when I touch her, the air around us can't even contain the excitement and breaks into sparks, I don't know. Why when I saw her in the store, in the front row of my own concert, in the dark alley, nothing else seems to focus and all I can see is her, I don't know. It just is.

When I opened my greenroom door to see the rosin box and my note laying there on the floor, discarded, I told myself to stop. Stop chasing her, stop thinking about her, stop wondering about what it would be like to be with her. Stop playing over and over the short but quippy conversations we'd had that had left my mind reeling and my body wanting.

And my resolve had held strong, and it had lasted...a night. And this morning, first thing, I had Hank drive me to the music store where it had all started and it had led me here.

I don't know why she didn't come see me last night.

But I am going to find out why, and I am going to change her mind.

***

The hallways are empty when I walk through them. I cringe a little at the latent smell of high school boy that's lingering and I wonder how many of these lockers house rotting sandwiches and month-old fruit.

I pass door after door, staring into abandoned classrooms, chairs left haphazardly around the room, dust still billowing in the air from cleaned blackboards. Five, six, seven rooms I've counted and still no Cadence to be seen.

But now, I can hear a soft tinkling from somewhere in the distance. It's so soft, it almost feels like I'm imagining it. But my brain recognizes it before I do, and as I make my way to the further classroom down the hall, I can hear myself humming along to the melody of "Fur Elise".

The door to the classroom is open, and the sound is crystal clear now. I don't have to look to know who's playing. It's her. It can only be her.

Her touch on the piano is exquisite, and I want to just close my eyes and let the music envelop itself around me. This piece that has been so overplayed, it's been relegated to almost a clichéd, banal experience, is coming alive to me like it hasn't in years. Somehow, she's made this composition, this elevator, phone hold, cell phone ringtone music sound like what it was originally supposed to be...a love song. "Fur Elise", for Elise...a music composed out of love, a gift from Beethoven to a beloved.

She breathes life, she imbues love back into it.

I creep to the doorway and peek around.

I watch her lost in her own performance. She's smiling softly and swaying slightly. Her eyes are closed and she seems so at peace. And I know what that feels like. But it thrills me to see it manifested in her as well.

This woman...she could understand me. When so many others have tried and failed.

The familiar song is coming to an end and I feel my face flush at the thought of confronting her.

Get it together man, I psych myself up. I can't remember the last time I was nervous talking to a woman, but everything feels new with her, and as if there's so much as stake.

The music ends and I step into the room, clapping gently.

She stiffens and then whips her head around.

She does NOT look happy to see me. In fact, her eyes are both cold and distant, but it looks like she's trying not to look angry at the same time.

I hadn't expected she'd roll out the red carpet, but I thought that it'd just been cold feet that had her leaving last night without seeing me. But it seems like something much, much more.

"Hi, Cadence." I still get a thrill out of saying her name. Like it ties me to her, knowing this information about her.

"What are you doing here?" She turns back to the piano, her back to me.

Her shortness stops me in my tracks. "You didn't come see me backstage last night," I state, hoping it would provoke her to tell me why. I can't see her face but I hear her take a breath. But no words follow. I take the chance to take a few steps closer to her. "So, I thought I'd come see you instead."

"How did you know where to find me?" Another question. This isn't turning out how I'd hoped, I thought I was going to be the one getting answers. But if it relaxed her, I could play this game for a while.

"George," I say, naming the music store owner.

"George?" She seems surprised at the name. "Oh. Right. The rosin."

"Yeah." One more step.

"So, last night? Why didn't you come see me?" I ask again. This woman's stubbornness is the stuff of legends.

"I did. I did see you."

"You did?" I think quickly but nothing comes to mind. "Where? I waited."

"You looked busy."

"Well, that's normal backstage, it's crazy back there. You should've just come up and interrupted me."

Her voice drops so low I can't quite make out the words. "You didn't look like you would appreciate being interrupted...with her, with that...woman."

"Woman?" What was she talking about?

"The woman you were hugging and kissing. Outside your dressing room door."

Oh my god. She saw me with-...Fuck! "Whoa, hang on Cadence, I can...um, shit. I can explain that."

"No." One word. Clear and firm.

"Just let me..." I scramble, I walk right up to her, hoping she'll let me clarify what happened.

"No!" She turns around to face me. The forcefulness of her refusal seems to shock her even more than me.

"Ok," I back off, holding my hands up in surrender.

"Sebastian," her voice wavers and I can tell whatever she seems to be struggling to say is both important and hard for her.

I let her take a breath, and take a risk and reach out, hooking my finger under her chin and lifting her to face me.

"Just say whatever you need to say. I'll listen."

My words seem to have an impact on her and she swallows and starts to talk.

"I. Just. Can't. Sebastian. Do this with you. Start anything. Your lifestyle, this band and you being who I imagine you are, you're going to break my heart. Last night, for a split second I thought I could handle it, and that I could just have some fun, but I can't. And I'm glad I saw what I saw, because it gave me a taste of what would be in store for me, and as hard as it was for me to see last night, it'll only be worse in a few days' or a week's or a month's time. So you don't need to explain or apologize about anything. Because it doesn't matter. This isn't going to go anywhere. I don't want it to."

I don't know what to say.

But I think I know enough about this weird, mysterious woman to know, nothing I say right now is going to change her mind.

So, I don't. I will give her time.

I move my finger away from her chin but she doesn't look away. Her gaze unsettles me, I expected her to turn away after the speech, but it seems to have emboldened her instead.

I pivot away from her and take a step toward the middle of the room.

"You conduct the orchestra?" I gesture to the semi-circle of chairs.

"Yes."

"How big is it?"

"Almost fifty students."

"Wow!" I'm honestly impressed. Even at my renowned music college, conducting a group of fifty is a task undertaken only by the best or the most committed. I knew she was talented, now I had a little sense of her tenacity and commitment.

"They any good?" I ask, expecting a humble response.

"They're the best," she answers, without missing a beat.

I can't help but laugh at the way she says it so matter of factly. She says it without an ounce of bragging. She actually thinks they are the best.

She just shrugs at my reaction and repeats her statement. "They are the best. They are motivated, hardworking, passionate and just plain talented."

"All of them?" I don't know why I'm questioning her; I think I just like to hear her speaking with such conviction.

"Sure. I mean, some more talented than others while others work harder than the naturally gifted ones."

"So, it's really the common factor maybe, that makes them the best."

"What's that?" she asks.

God, she doesn't even see it.

"You."

Her face flares red in an instant and she turns back to her piano, which I'm starting to realize is her security blanket. I have one too, my cello.

"You play beautifully." I realize I haven't told her yet.

"No, YOU play beautifully," she sighs and I wish I had a recording of the sound.

And then I tell her what I've been thinking since I walked into the school grounds. "You're too good for this place, Cadence."

She doesn't say anything and just turns on her creaky piano stool and follows my eyes around the room. The dark, decaying room with the falling apart music stands and the stained carpet. The dusty shelf of music scores held together by browning masking tape that would crumble under a strong breath. I watch her sitting there, like an angel amongst ghetto ruins. The only light in the place.

"You should be teaching...or performing in some of the best schools, the best concert halls in the world. Trust me. I've been in them. You wouldn't be out of place."

"So, you mean where there would be other teachers just like me?" her voice asks quietly.

"Yes! Really, really talented musicians. The best there are. From all over the world. You'd beat them all out, all those people vying for a place there. Killing themselves and each other for a chance there."

"Hmmm." She grows pensive for a few moments, then speaks up again, "Oh. So, can I ask you a question?"

"Sure." I'm thrilled that's she's engaging with me.

"You're saying those places are filled with amazing teachers? Musicians? The best of the best?"

"That's exactly what I'm saying." And hoping she'll believe.

"Then *why* would they need *me*?"

Well, that shut me up.

I had never thought of it that way before. Probably because I'm a selfish bastard.

"Wow. I didn't even think…"

"It's okay. It was sweet, thank you." And she gifts me with the sweetest smile I've ever seen in my life. "Thank you for thinking that I could have a chance at such amazing places as those. That you think I could do better. But that exact want for me to have something better? That's exactly how I feel about my kids."

Her sincerity touches me and I feel warmed by her giving spirit.

"It's too bad that not everyone sees it that way, though," she adds.

"What do you mean?"

"Nothing." She sounds embarrassed that she's said it.

"No, tell me." I urge her softly.

"Well, it just looks like we're not going to have enough money to take the kids to Nationals in Canberra. We just don't have the money."

"Canberra?"

"Oh, I forgot, most people don't know that Canberra is the capital city of Australia. It's where the National School Orchestra Competition is held."

"How much would it cost?"

"Thousands. Thousands we don't have and don't have enough time to raise. For the bus, for accommodations. For the entry fees. A lot of miscellaneous costs you couldn't imagine. Thousands…it might as well be millions." It's the first time, other than when she declared that there was never going to be anything between us, that she sounds like she's given up.

"So – what will happen?" I ask, honestly interested.

"What do you think?"

I shake my head. "I don't know."

Strangely, she grins at me and it's nice to see the life light up back in her. "You've been a privileged meeeeeeeeeellionaire too long. What happens when you can't afford something? You just don't do it!"

"Well, that seems wrong." I said plainly.

She laughs, "Change that to 'unfair' and you'll sound just like my kids."

"I like me already." I say haughtily.

"Well, yeah, most people like hanging around with people the same mental age as themselves," she chuckles.

I turn to her, trying to look insulted. But seeing the light dance in her eyes makes me burst into laughter as I shrug, surrendering, "Hey, when you're right, you're right."

Our laughter dies down and it's quiet in the room, but not awkward. I'm watching her as she looks around the room, and I can see pride on her face. She's built something here, I feel. Probably something like the pride I feel when I see our CDs on display or walk past our promo posters. Something tangible that documents the success, the result of all our hard work.

"Did you enjoy the concert last night?" I don't want to stir up her ill feelings about last night, but I'm hoping she won't mind talking about the performance.

She turns completely around on the piano stool, tucking her hands under her legs. She doesn't answer immediately, but it doesn't make me worry. It looks like she's trying to find the right words.

"It...it wasn't what I expected," her words are slow and measured.

Well, that makes me a little nervous...what HAD she expected?

"I didn't know what to expect from 'classical music mashed with rock'," she continues, a look of confusion spreads now across her brow.

I can't help but laugh. "I know, right? Who came up with that brilliant description?"

She seems to relax at my response, as if she was worried about offending me. "It just doesn't seem like the right way to describe it."

"How would you describe it?"

"I would...I don't know," she stops.

"No, it's okay, it can't be worse than 'classical mashed rock'. It sounds like a side dish for an early bird special at the pub on a Thursday night."

The sound of her unbridled laughter makes me want to repeat what I said, just to draw it out a little longer.

"Well, I'd go with something a little more elegant. Contemporary Chamber Rock maybe? It could tie in your style a little more elegantly than mashed potato rock classics or whatever it is now. So, the contemporary would cover the modern music you do, and the concept of 'chamber music' in the description would suggest classical music too."

I sigh. Of course, she would get it.

"But anyway, whatever you call it – last night was...it was life affirming."

I had heard it all before – all the words describing our performance, but that one was and I imagine, will always be, my favorite.

"It affirmed to me, that music is essential to beauty, to life," she adds.

And in this moment I don't know whether to propose to her, or bend her over that piano and show her just how life affirming I can be.

"Ha, I even got the kids to warm up to a jam session playing "Bitter Sweet Symphony" and let them experiment with blending it with some Beethoven this afternoon."

"And?"

"They loved it! They've already come up with a list of songs we could try mashing together in our next jam session."

"NO! We don't need any competition!"

"Well, you've got it, buster!"

We grin at each other. Connecting over this common passion.

And then it comes to me. I jump up a little, just on the spot, I'm so excited.

"Cadence? I have a proposition for you."

"Sebastian, I already-..."

"No, hear me out. This has nothing to do with you and me, it's actually a favor for the band."

"Ok."

"And the school."

"I'm listening."

"You know we're here for a few months, right?"

"No."

"Well, we are, for about ten weeks. We're here to work on the arrangements and record our next album."

I wait for her to nod before continuing.

"Well, we need a pianist for a few of our tracks. We didn't bring one with us, but over the last few days we've been wanting to open up the sound to about three or four of our new tracks."

"No." She knows where I'm going and she shakes her head.

"Hang on...don't say no yet. It won't be a huge commitment, but you'll be perfect for it. And when we're done... when it's done, I will donate $50 000 to the school's music program. That should get you to Canberra and back. For the next few years, I imagine."

She gasps.

I need to hit while the iron's hot. "For a few hours a week rehearsing and recording over the next ten weeks. For $50 000. What do you say?"

She just shakes her head and I can't believe she's refusing.

"Don't say 'no' without seriously thinking about this Cadence." I warn her.

She just stares at me, openmouthed. "But, why? Why would you do this?"

"Because we need someone like you to remind us why we're all in this, and why we got into this in the first place."

"Sebastian."

"Look, you don't have to answer right away." Especially if your answer is going to be no, I tell myself.

"Ok."

"How 'bout now?" I ask again quickly.

She gives me a look that probably has her kids shaking in their school shoes. The effect on me is higher up my body, and I have to bite my tongue to stop it.

"Just think about it." I hand her a piece of paper with my number on it. I ignore the spark that shoots up my arm when she takes it from my fingers. I don't expect any less now when I touch her. "And let me know, Mary."

"Why-?"

I lean in and whisper in her ear, "You'll have to call to find out."

And stealing one last look, I walk out the door and wonder if I'll ever hear from her again.

Chapter Nine

CADENCE

"I have conditions," I say when he opens the door to his hotel room three hours later. He sent a car when I called to say I wanted to talk and it's brought me here.

I try to ignore the fact that he broke out into a huge grin as soon as he saw me. Fixating on that's just going to make the swarm of butterflies in my stomach take flight. And I have to remind them, that this is just about the school and the kids.

"Come in and have a drink," he reaches his hand out, and I pull back.

"Um, is there somewhere else we can talk? A little more out in the open?" I'm not sure which one of us I don't trust when it comes to us being alone.

"Sure, but you can pay for the drinks then. In here, you can have anything, everything you want. And trust me, I have everything."

Something about him makes me constantly want to challenge him, so I ask. "What about some Choyo?" I name a Japanese plum wine.

"You want that heated up or cold?" he asks, without missing a beat, and turns back into the room towards a drinks cart.

I follow him, as if lured into the room by a magnetic force drawing me to him. "You have it?"

"Cadence, when are you going to stop questioning me?" He winks and pours a glass of wine and brings it over to me, taking my bag and jacket and laying them down on the couch.

The lounge of his suite is almost as big as my entire apartment. An entire side is windows and looks out to the Sydney city skyline. It's a view I don't see often, and it's breathtaking. I walk over to press my hand against the glass, it's cold and I pull my hand back, knocking the glass in my other hand over.

"Oh shit, I'm so sorry!" I bend over to pick up the glass but he's already there, taking it from my hands and pushing them away as I try to mop up the spill with the napkin he'd slipped under the glass.

"Don't worry about it! It'll just blend in with all the other drink spills I leave behind."

Something about the opulence of the room has me a little unnerved and it takes me a little while to notice he's still holding my hand.

I pull it away, and he looks a little surprised, hurt.

"Oh, I'm sorry, you just looked a little shaken up. I didn't mean anything by it."

"It's okay. Um, let's just get back to those conditions?"

"Yes, ma'am!" He sits down on the couch and gestures to the seat next to him.

I grab my bag and settle down in the settee across from him, and try to sound as confident as I can negotiating a deal that's more money than I've ever had to handle.

"So, I have four conditions and I want them in a signed contract – "

"Ok, name 'em."

"Firstly, the rehearsal and recording time can't interfere with my normal work at the school, which is mostly school hours and some Saturday time."

"Done. We are night owls, we can practice at any time."

"Oh. okay, good. Um, two. I imagine that you normally would pay a musician for playing on your record, an hourly rate or fixed rate or whatever –"

"Yes."

"But since you've agreed to the donation amount to the school, that will be the entirety of my fee."

"Hang on a minute – that's not fair to you."

"No discussion. Yes, or I walk right now."

"Cadence."

I cock an eyebrow. It's a well-weathered teacher's 'don't cross me' eyebrow, and it seems to work on cocky musicians as well.

"Fine."

"Three. I want to audition for the rest of the band and make sure they're going to be okay with this."

"They're fine. I wouldn't make this deal if I didn't think they'd be okay with it."

"Well, good. Then they can tell me themselves when I audition."

He just shrugs.

"And four. This is a purely professional transaction. We are not going to fall madly in love or lust. I told you before, Sebastian. I am not interested in anything personal with you. If you pursue anything, I'm out. "

He gets up from the couch and I can't figure out if I've offended him or amused him. He turns toward the view for a moment, running his hands up and down his legs and then back to me.

"What did he do to you?"

"Who he did what?" I ask, confused.

"Who made you so afraid of men that you need to put it in a legal contract to ensure you'll stay away from me?"

I stare at him openmouthed. I can't believe the audacity of this guy. But I can't deny it...he's got style.

"It's to make you stay away from me!" I tell him, not without a little hope it'll bruise his healthy ago.

"A contract's not going to do that, Cadence. You know there's something here between us. Words on a piece of paper aren't going to make that miraculous feeling fade away."

"No, but it might ensure that we don't act on it." I'm hardly even convincing myself at this point.

"Are you really that weak? Do you think that I am?"

"Do you agree to the terms or not, Sebastian?"

There's a pause, and I wonder if I've pushed him too far. I don't know this man, I don't know his limits, I don't even really know his motives. I want this deal. I just want it on my terms. Unfortunately, I think I've come to the wrong man for that.

"I will, if you answer the question." He makes sure I'm looking at him before he repeats the question, "What asshole thing did your last partner do that has you running so scared?"

I know I have to give him some answer. But he hasn't earned the right to the whole story yet.

"Everything you're doing now. And more. Charmed me, chased me, then made me regret I ever laid eyes on him."

"I won't do that." He shakes his head as emphasis.

"He said that too."

"You want to put it in the contract?" He grins, finding the ridiculousness of it all.

"That we're not going to pursue a personal relationship? Yes!" I throw my hands up, frustrated.

"No, that I won't turn into a dick-knuckle."

I can't help but spit my drink out as I guffaw.

"What? I won't!" he insists.

"That's because…because… dick-knuckle is not a thing!" I can barely get out over my laughter.

"Fine, I won't be a dick, asshole, sleazebag. Whatever boring word you want to use."

"Yes, because…. it's not going to come to that. I won't let it. And … the deal's off if it does." I glare at him, and for a moment, our eyes battle for a win.

Then holding my gaze, he walks up so close to me, I'm afraid he can hear my heart thump. He reaches around my back and pulls me into him. My face is almost buried in his chest so I tip my chin and rest it against his sternum, forcing my eyes to lock on his. I've spent so much time trying not to stare at him, it's the first time I notice the swirl of brown through his bottomless jade green eyes. His eyelashes are ridiculously thick and lush and I bite my lip trying not to reach out and touch them with my fingertips.

He's not smiling but his lips are slightly open and up close I can see how far the scar on his upper lip dips into his top lip. It's quivering a little and I wonder what the point of all this is.

But I don't have to wonder for long.

"Deal, but only if you let me kiss you. Just once."

SEBASTIAN

If there was ever a moment I belonged in a straitjacket, it would be this moment right now.

What am I doing, giving her an ultimatum to kiss me?

I'm not sure what came over me, but I just couldn't bear the thought that there might never be something between us. It's not what I had planned when I'd gone to see her today, and definitely not what I had expected would happen if we spent ten weeks together. But she hadn't given me a chance to explain about last night, and the only way I could think of to get her to spend more time with me, was through this deal.

So here we are.

And she is looking so goddamned fuckable I want to just press her against the window and have the whole of Sydney watch me make her mine. But she's not having it. So fine, I will agree to her plan, but I'm going to make her remember this moment for the next ten weeks. I want it keeping her up at nights, like I know it's already got me up.

Her body stiffens as I pull my face away from her, even as my arms come around to circle her waist and I nudge my hips against her.

"Just one kiss, Cadence. And I'll agree to everything," I whisper against her ear.

I can see a twitch in her jaw, and it's driving me crazy not to drag my lips along it. Her skin is translucent and fine like a glass doll's, and her body feels soft, warm, pliable in my hands. Like I could mold her into any shape I wanted, and play her like my own human cello. Oh god, the sounds I could make come from her...making her come.

"Sebastian," she chokes softly on my name.

And I don't give her a chance to continue.

I lower my mouth to hers, surprised to find her lips moist and open, inviting. *Yes, show me you want this as much as I do, Cadence*, the thought loops in my head. My hands travel down her back to her ass and pull her in hard against me. She moans a little, an escape of desire dislodging from the back of her throat and vibrating against my mouth. It sends my blood wild. My lips spread her lips open wider and my tongue slips into her mouth; her tongue is waiting and it flicks against the tip of mine. I can't help but grind my hips against her and I know she can feel my hardness straining against my jeans and pressing into the softness of her stomach.

"Cadence," I think I moan, and she touches my face in response.

Finally, we pull away, our breaths hissing through our teeth as we stare at each other over our panting.

I don't know what's stopping me from picking her up and taking her to my bedroom and making her emit that moan over and over again, but the sight of her lipstick slightly smudged over those full, luscious lips and her tits rising and falling, daring me to bury my face in their fleshy pillows, isn't helping.

I take a step towards her. And she takes a step back, holding her hand up to stop me.

"One kiss. That was the deal," she says, her voice wavering.

"Cadence."

"One kiss. First and last."

"If that's what you want."

She doesn't say yes. But she doesn't say no.

This is insane. I run my hand through my hair to stop from grabbing her around the neck and pulling her lips to mine again.

She takes a step back, and I'm almost thankful for the physical distance.

"Wh- where's the lady's room, please?"

I point her to the half-bath in the adjoining room. And she walks off, my eyes glued to the gentle sway of her ass as she leaves.

This woman is driving me fucking crazy.

I grab the largest glass on the bar and fill it with cognac, downing it in one drink, welcoming the distraction of the searing heat down my throat and churning my stomach.

I hear the tap turn off in the other room and I grab my jacket, waiting for her at the door.

She comes out, and there's no sign of our kiss except for my softening cock and the way her eyes can't meet mine.

"Come on then," I gesture to the door with my head. She responds with a look of confusion.

"You wanted to audition, let's go get you auditioned. The guys are in the rehearsal room down the hall."

I open the door and she steps through it, adjusting the belt on her dress, and I try not to notice how it sits just on the curve of her ass, her firm but cushiony ass that was just in my hands.

This is going to be an interesting ten weeks.

Chapter Ten

CADENCE

It's a silent walk as we walk down the long, softly lit hallway of the Shangri-La Hotel to the band's rehearsal room. I'm a little too afraid to speak in case I either beg him to kiss me again or tell him the deal is off. Five minutes in the bathroom was really only enough to touch up my lipstick and do a silent scream to let out the frustration of not jumping him there and then. I can't remember when I have had such a physical response to someone. Sex has always been paired with an emotional connection for me, but after only knowing him for a day, surely there's no emotional connection to be had here, I simply want to fuck him. Every time he looks at me with those marbled green and brown eyes, I feel hypnotized, like at the click of his fingers, my body is his to do with at his bidding.

Before I came here, I thought the contract would help us both stay on track, but that was before I knew what I would be missing. Now that I do, I wonder what I've set myself up for.

Which I imagine was just his intent.

Dick-knuckle, indeed.

"Cadence," I hear him say my name and I stop. He's standing at a door a few feet back, I hadn't even noticed him stopping.

"They're in here." He cocks his head and smiles. "You ready?"

"You make it sound like I should be scared."

"Hey, you're the one who wanted to audition. Not my fault they're like piranhas picking off lousy musicians-..."

Fuck, what've I gotten myself in for? "Wha-?"

"I'm just kidding! They're gonna love you."

He doesn't give me a moment to rethink before he opens the door and gestures for me to enter the room.

Sebastian closes the door behind me and we step into the lounge of a similar room to his, except that there are instruments and audio equipment everywhere. Amongst it all are five males, three I recognize as part of the band, an older man about forty-five and a younger guy in his late teens.

"Guys, this is Cadence." Sebastian waves in my direction, and sits down on an empty spot on the couch.

I feel like I'm on display, with the five sets of eyes staring me down. I wring my hands and they feel cold and clammy.

"Er, yeah, hi, guys," I hear my voice speak out and I do a lame wave. *Yeah, that'll impress them,* my inner bitch voice snickers.

Sebastian chuckles a little, obviously sensing my discomfort and I want to wring his neck. I throw him a look which must convey my desperation, because he gets up and stands next to me again.

"Cadence is here to audition for the piano part that we need in those new songs we're doing for the album."

"Oh," Jez stands up and comes over to me, "I thought he was introducing you for another reason." He winks and I realize he remembers me from last night in the alley.

"Oooh, what other reason? Do tell!" A guy I recognize as the violinist draped on the love seat pipes up. "We love us some gossip."

"There's no gossip!" I snap defensively and the violinist grins back at me.

"Ignore him," Sebastian says to me and pushes me gently over to the keyboard. "It's not a Steinway, but it'll do what you need," he says softly to me, trying to relax me, except that his proximity is doing the exact opposite.

I sit down and run my fingers over the keys, testing their sensitivity and working the pedal.

"You've got the job!" Jez calls out, and I have to laugh, smiling at him appreciatively for breaking the tension. "Ha, just take it easy, none of us are piano players here, so you've got nothing to worry about."

"Hey! I play a little piano!" Brad says, sounding insulted.

"You need a repertoire ranging more than chopsticks and "Frere Jacques" to be considered a true piano player, ballsack!" s fourth voice speaks up from a corner way in the back.

"That's Marius, he's our violinist, when he's not sitting on his head and preaching veganism while eating a chicken drumstick," Sebastian explains.

"Fuck you! I said I was going to convert...one day!" Marius counters.

I rub my hands together and let their banter sink in and relax me.

"Um, what do you want me to play?" I ask.

"Whatever you like. Whatever it is, Dennis will hate it anyway." Jez grins and then clenches his jaw as if bracing for something. That something is a toy foam football that comes hurtling towards his head from the direction of the older guy.

"Dennis is our manager. He hates music, traveling and well, us. But we make him rich so he tolerates it." Brad tells me, and I'm glad he's moved his teasing on to someone else.

I turn to look at Dennis who just shrugs and goes back to his tablet.

Their banter is relentless and I feel intimidated by the bond they have, a bond that was obvious on-stage last night. And not for the first time I think that I'm way out of my league playing with them. Last night, on stage, they were like a four-limbed, stringed mythical creature, sounding battle cries and sweet nothings in the form of epic ballads and rock anthems. How was I going to compete, or even match up to that?

I turn to look at Sebastian, who smiles and squeezes my shoulder. It burns where he touches me even after he pulls away and I take the chance to distract myself from him by thinking of what to play.

I rest my fingers on the keys for a moment, closing my eyes, and as always hearing the opening stanzas in my head before I start.

Then I press down and let the music speak for itself.

I choose to open with Chopin's – "Ballade" in G minor. It has a dramatic opening and a wonderfully expressive introduction. I keep my eyes closed and try to forget everything that's around me. Then something in the notes reminds of the song "Say Something" by A Great Big World. I slowly transition between the classical piece and this iconic modern ballad.

As the chorus breaks, I feel the guys move around me, but I don't dare open my eyes in case I break my connection to the song. And then I hear a soft cello string note sound, harmonizing with my song. Then one by one, the second cello, and the violin and then viola join in. Each finding their own notes, weaving in and out around mine. I can't help but smile as it's no longer a piano solo, but a small symphony of sound. I switch to a higher octave and hear Sebastian's cello fill the space I've left, taking the lead, the melody strong and beautiful in his hands.

Then as the piece descends to its close, the violin and viola drop away, then Jez's cello and finally it's just me and Sebastian. Playing the same notes but on instruments created from different worlds. I hold my breath as I play the last note, holding it as long as it takes before the sound fades away from Sebastian's bow.

I feel my lungs empty, not realizing I'd been holding my breath. I wait for someone to say something, but there's no sound, only the noise of the guys putting down their instruments.

And then Dennis speaks up, "And then there were five."

The guys burst out into laughter and I can't help but still sit there stunned.

"Cadence!" Jez comes up and pats me on the back. "You are fucking brilliant, just what we've been looking for! Where have you been all our lives?"

Sebastian looks over at me and smiles, "I've been wondering that myself."

"We have to put this mashup on our album. We'll play around with it a bit, is that okay with you Cadence?" Jez asks, already jotting something down on a piece of paper.

"Er, yeah, sure, it's just something that came to me just then," I tell him honestly.

"You are perfect for us," Brad says as peers over Jez's shoulder.

"Eh, you're all right, I guess," Marius shrugs as he hands me a bottle of water. "Not too bad for a piano teacher."

"Spoken like a true failed piano student," I can't help but rib him, feeling more comfortable now that they've accepted me somewhat.

"Oohhhhh!" the rest of the band laughs as Marius pretends to hang his head.

"Oh, and by the way," Sebastian speaks up, "What do you think of this for our new band name...The Rock Chamber Boys?"

They all go quiet and then grin at each other and whoop, lifting their hands in a series of high fives.

"That's fucking it. That's exactly what we've been looking for." Brad says. "Who thought of it?"

"Our new pianist," Sebastian points to me and winks.

"Dennis, you better watch out, or else you're going to be out of a job. Leaving us to find our own pianist, and now her coming up with our band name." Jez shakes his finger at his manager.

"I'm not worried, dickheads."

"Why not?"

"Because I have more drunk pictures of you fuckwits doing idiotic shit than I need to keep me in blackmail millions for the rest of my life."

"Touché."

We all laugh and barely hear the knock on the door until Jez yells "Come in, it's open!"

The door opens and in walks the tall blonde from last night.

SEBASTIAN

I knew she'd be a hit.

From the first note of the Chopin piece, I saw the guys eyeing each other, to the way she led us into the transition of the ballad and instinctively knew how to mold the sounds, the harmonies, something we'd taken years of playing together to learn.

Her music pulls at my heart and her body and mind tugs on my dick. I want her so bad at this moment, I'm glad the other guys are in the room to stop me from doing something stupid and scaring her off.

I watch her blending in with the banter and I wonder what it'd be like for her to join us permanently. She'd bring some class to the place, that's for sure.

Dennis says something and I barely hear him, just watching her laugh along.

"Come in, it's open!" Jez yells towards the door and I hadn't even noticed someone was knocking.

The door open and Hailey walks in, carrying some shopping bags and drops onto the empty spot on the couch next to me.

"Hey, guys, what's going on? What are we laughing that?" She reaches over me to the snack plate on the coffee table and pushes my legs out of the way.

"Dennis is threatening to out us all as pathetic drunks on TMZ so he can keep affording his designer coffees and pedicures," Brad explains, and Hailey rolls her eyes and throws a cheese ball at Dennis' head.

I notice Cadence stand up in the corner of my eyes and head towards the door. I get up and join her just as she reaches for the handle.

"Hey, where are you going?" I ask her.

She doesn't look at me and presses down on the door handle.

"Hey. You okay?" I touch her gently on her shoulder and she jerks away from, still not answering, a small hiss emitting from her lips.

She turns to the room and clears her throat, "Um, guys, I've gotta go now. Give me a call when you're ready to rehearse. Thanks again for the chance."

"Ok, see ya, Cadence!" the guys shout out and she gives them a quick wave before pulling the door open and walking out.

I follow her, but she's fast, pretty much running down the hall to my hotel room.

"Hey! Cadence, wait! What's going on?" I catch up with her at my hotel room and she stands there staring at it, as if trying to burn a hole through it with her glare.

"Can you please let me in so I can grab my stuff and go home? It's late and I have an early meeting before class." Her voice is cold and hard. I haven't heard it like this before.

"Hey," I touch her softly on the shoulder again, and she whips around and glares at me.

"Don't. Touch me. Again."

"Hey, hey...What happened?" I don't know what's happened in the last few minutes that's caused a complete change in her demeanor.

"Sebastian, just open the door."

"Not until you tell me what's going on?"

"Nothing."

"Cade-..."

"Just, I didn't expect to see her there. okay? Just drop it?"

"Who?"

"The woman from last night," she hisses through her teeth and leans her head against the door.

Oh my god, I'm such a fucking idiot. I can't believe I didn't make the connection.

"Oh, Cadence, I'm so sorry, I didn't realize...That's Hailey...She's..." I try to choose the right words.

"No! I don't want to know. I told you at the school this afternoon and I'm telling you now, I don't care." She turns her head to avoid my eyes.

"Cadence...come on," I lower my voice, wanting to comfort her.

"Open the door, Sebastian."

I ignore her, and press her against the door, my hands wrapped around her arms, forcing her to look at me. She struggles slightly, but doesn't look away.

"Cadence, her name is Hailey. She's Dennis' daughter. I've known her for ten years. She's like a sister to me. There's nothing going on between us, never has been never, never will be."

She narrows her eyes and takes a breath. "I don't care, Sebastian."

"I think you do, Cadence. Contract or no contract, you care. So that's the truth. What you saw last night, was just me seeing her for the first time in almost a year. She's been at school while we've been on tour. We're all really close."

"Fuck, Sebastian! Why did you tell me that?" My hands are still around her biceps but she somehow manages to lift her forearms and thump on my chest with her fists.

"Because I'm not going to have you hating me when I did nothing to deserve it." She turns her face and I follow her gaze, forcing her to look me in the eye again. I can feel the heat rise through her body to her cheeks. "Hate your ex-boyfriend, hate the real assholes who hurt you, but don't lump me in with them when I did nothing to deserve it." The pain in her eyes tell me there's a story behind all this. A heartbreaking past. A hurt I don't deserve to know yet.

Her fists fall to her sides and she sighs, "Sebastian. I... I just can't."

She becomes limp against the door and I wonder how easy it would be to scoop her up in my arms. But I don't.

"Ok. If you don't want to give us a chance, fine. But it's not because I didn't try. When you want to hate me, at least do it for the things I did and not the things you think I would do."

I let her go and she lets out a breath before asking me, "Why are you doing this?"

"What?"

"This. All of it. Hiring me as the piano player when you could get anyone, people way more talented and less trouble. And the money, the donation. It's so much money. Why?"

"I have my reasons."

"Tell me one."

I breathe. No point in hiding it.

"You."

Her breath catches in her throat. I can't tell if it's the answer she wanted or feared. Or both. But there was no use lying about it. She smiles softly at me and presses a soft hand on my chest. My heart threatens to jump out of my chest to be cradled in her palm.

"This isn't going to work, is it?" She smiles at me sadly.

"Yes, it will. The guys love you, they're not going to let you go now. And anyway, I've gotten my one kiss. So now, now we move on." I give her a resigned smile.

I reach around her and open the door to my hotel room. And try not to bury my face in her hair.

"Take as long as you need, when you're ready the car will be waiting for you downstairs. Dennis will call you tomorrow about a rehearsal schedule."

"I'm sorry, Sebastian."

"Me too, Cadence." I lean in and kiss her softly on the cheek and walk away.

Chapter Eleven

CADENCE

"Fuck, I'm tired. Can we take a break yet?" Marius sighs at the end of the song and collapses into a nearby chair.

"Dude, we've been rehearsing for like five minutes." Brad pokes him with the tip of his bow.

"Nuh-uh!"

"Um, okay, eight," Brad corrects himself.

"Exactly, seven's my limit before I need a break, you know that."

"I thought that was just with sex," Sebastian teases him.

"You're thinking of Brad. I'm tantric, remember?"

"Blue balls are not the same as tantric."

"Sure feels like it," Marius laments.

"Break's over!" Dennis yells from his seat at the dining table, not bothering to look up.

Jez winks at me and I can't help but giggle at the banter. The band has been so supportive during my first few rehearsals, patient with me stumbling through the new songs, some I haven't even heard of before. But it's been so exciting, I can't wait for rehearsal days and stay up nights practicing my parts and thinking of ways to improve. It's been so long since I've played in any sort of performance capacity and even longer as part of an ensemble, I'm almost drunk on the adrenaline of creating music.

This opportunity of playing on this album is so incredible, I feel like I've fallen under a lucky wishing star and all my dreams are being granted.

Except for one.

Sebastian has kept his promise so far, and since our one and only kiss, he hasn't come closer than within a few feet to me. He is friendly and treats me like one of the guys but hasn't touched me or said anything remotely suggestive to me. There's no sign of the burning need from that night outside his hotel room door.

Well, they do say, be careful what you wish for.

"Cadence?" Sebastian says my name, and I wonder how long I've been daydreaming.

"Oh, sorry."

"You okay? Why don't you take a break?" he asks me, a little concerned.

"Hey! How come she gets a break?" Marius grumbles as he gets back on his feet.

"She's just come straight from working with high school kids for eight hours. You woke up twenty minutes ago after a twelve-hour nap," Jez reminds him.

"Also, she's prettier," Brad grins and winks at me.

"Ha, I don't know about that," I admit. I might be many things but I was definitely not as beautiful as these guys. "Do you all go to the same plastic surgeon or something?" I ask, it'd be hard to pick who was better looking out of the four. But that doesn't stop me from still having my favorite.

"Excuse me, this is all au naturel," Sebastian huffs, sticking his nose up in the air and caressing his chiseled cheeks.

It sure does look God-given to me. I turn my focus back to the music to stop my thoughts drifting back to how it felt with his body pressed up hard against me.

"Did no one hear me when I said 'break's over'?" Dennis yells at us again and we try to hold in our laughter as long as possible before Jez breaks down and bursts out in a huge guffaw, sending the rest of us into a huge giggle fit.

These last few days have been the most fun I've had in years.

And then, just like that, it's back to business. All jokes and messing around about aside, these guys are truly hardcore, hardworking musicians and they take their art so seriously. It makes my heart sing to be learning so much from them.

***

An hour and a half later, we decide that we've done enough for the day. Hank, Sebastian's assistant, hands me a bottle of water and I down it in almost one gulp. I hadn't realized how thirsty I was.

"Fuck, it's really coming down out there," Brad says, leaning against the window, taking a big bite out of his routine post-rehearsal apple.

We all herd over to the window, watching the sky open up and spill a heaven of tears onto the Sydney metropolis. The layers of gray and white interweaving are mesmerizing and we stand in awe of the power of Mother Nature for a moment, feeling small and inconsequential.

"Nutfuckles!" The expletive breaks the mood and everybody turns to face me. It seems their creative potty-mouth tendencies have rubbed off on me.

Jez sighs and pats Sebastian on the arm. "And to think she was such a lady when you introduced her to us."

Sebastian grins and winks at me, and for a moment we're back in George's music shop, crammed in the back with me chastising him for swearing. I blush at the memory and avoid his look by rushing over to the couch to grab my bag and phone.

"Wassup, potty-mouth?" The guys follow me.

"I forgot that my friend Sarah drove me here today and I was going to walk home because it looked like such a nice day." I point to drenched sky. "I should work for the Channel 9 weather team."

"Oh, one of our cars can take you home," Dennis offers generously.

"Drivers are on their break," Hank tells us.

"I'll drive! I haven't driven for aaaages, I miss it!" Marius stands up and nudges me with his elbow. "You trust me, dontcha?"

I'm not sure I do but I appreciate the offer, and Sebastian has suddenly turned eerily quiet, so I nudge him back and say, "Of course, you should be bright and alert considering you've been sleeping for the last two hours."

"Nutfuckles, indeed," he responds and pushes me out the door. In the corner of my eye I can see Sebastian watching me. I give him a small wave and mouth, 'good night'. He barely smiles in response.

I guess he hasn't had any problem leaving it all behind after all.

***

"So, just before we go, which one is the gas pedal and which is the brake again?" Marius asks me.

"Marius!" I cry out, horrified.

"Relax, just kidding! I'm from London, remember? We drive on the left as well."

"Oh yeah, I forget you're from all over the world." I clasp my seatbelt and hold on probably tighter than I need to.

"Yup, Brad and I are from England, Jez is from Romania and Sebbie's a stinky Frenchman. But we've pretty much all lived in the UK since we were pretty young." He reminds me as he turns out of the parking lot and onto the main road.

"How did you all meet?"

"Well, we were all at the Guildhall School of Music in London together. At one point or another I guess we kept finding each other in detention and decided we might as well do something with our time together. We formed No Strings Attached, now Rock Chamber Boys," he gives me a quick wink before continuing, "... when we were about seventeen. There've been some member changes, at one point there were seven of us. But us four, we've always been the core and I guess that's partly why we wanted the name change, to really cement who are now as people and musicians."

"Marius. I think that's the longest you've ever spoken without saying a swear word," I tease him.

"Well, fuck me, if you ain't bloody right!!" he exclaims and we both get the giggles.

The laughs die down and we drive in silence for a while, watching the rain engulf the car.

I take advantage of him being quiet for a change and say what I've wanted to say for a while. "Hey, thanks for being so nice to me. You guys have...you've just made this very easy for me."

"Don't mention it. We're pretty simple, mate. Don't fuck with us and we won't fuck with you."

I just smile. I've been around them enough to know that they're all about mate ship and loyalty. There's nothing I could say that will mean as much as what I do.

We drive for a moment longer before he speaks up again, "I know about the $50,000."

"Ah. I was wondering if he was ever going to mention it."

"I don't know if the others know. But he let it slip to me a few days ago."

"Maybe he's regretting it." I shrug. "I don't know why he's doing it in the first place. It's crazy, he doesn't even know the kids."

Marius swerves sharply, cutting the traffic off and stopping suddenly by the side.

"What the-?" I gasp.

Marius cuts me off, "Don't question him. That's just the guy he is, Cadence. There's no ulterior motive here. You'll hurt him if you think otherwise. Trust me. He can't give his money away fast enough. He grew up hard, Cadence. Like, on the streets hard. And now he's just trying to give back. Half of our staff are people he grew up with, family and friends, and random people he's met on the street who just needed a second chance. If he sees someone he can help, he'll help them. No credit, no thanks necessary."

It takes me a moment to absorb everything he's said.

After a moment, I nudge him with my elbow and wink playfully, "Did he pay you to say all this?"

Marius guffaws, "Please, he couldn't afford me. I make just as much as he does and I have more saved since I'm not burdened by a burning need to do good."

I don't believe that for a moment, but I don't say anything, knowing he's just trying to make a point.

"Thanks for telling me."

"No problem." He turns back into the traffic.

"Anything else he didn't tell you to tell me that I might need to know?" I take the chance to get some inside info.

"Ah, now that stuff is probably gonna cost you, but like I said, you couldn't afford me." Marius grins and reaches for the car radio dial.

Chapter Twelve

SEBASTIAN

It's been two weeks since we started rehearsals for the new album, and I think I deserve some sort of medal for keeping my hands off of Cadence. Almost ten rehearsal sessions of me sitting there alternating between thinking of taking her in every position known to red-blooded mankind and then visualizing Weird Al Yankovic in a teddy and rotting meat to stop the effect that thinking of fucking her has on my cock.

Every sound, every word, every move she makes drives me fucking insane. The way her hair falls down her back, the soft bounce of her hips when she walks, her ass swaying to the music on the piano stool. Every little movement is torture to me. And she's the only one who can relieve it.

Is this the age-old effect of just not getting what you want? Because if it is, with this contract in place, I can't see me getting any relief any time soon.

It doesn't help that the other guys adore her. Because now I couldn't get rid of her if I tried. She's hardworking, passionate and just as talented as any of us. After long days at work, she comes and works until one of us begs Dennis to let us stop; never complaining, never stopping. Every rehearsal, she walks in here having taken everything we've suggested on board and worked on it. And every rehearsal she walks out, and I have to do everything in my power not to chase after her. Tell her, beg her not to leave.

Sometimes I also visualize me throwing her over my shoulder and dragging her back to my room like a caveman, but mostly, I just want to be with her, around her. Around her infectious endless positivity, her sharp and bright outlook on life.

She's done exactly what I'd hoped she would, breathe life back into our band. Reminding us how lucky we are to be doing what we're doing, and the life it allows us.

A few nights ago, almost falling asleep exhausted from our rehearsal schedule, I let the deal slip to Marius. Surprisingly, he didn't find it too shocking All he said was, "Good thing she can actually play."

Well, that and, "Don't fuck it up."

If he means professionally, well, that's up to her.

If he means personally, I think it's too late for that.

***

"Sebastian, can I talk to you alone for a moment?" Cadence comes up to me after we've packed up our instruments for the day. It's the first time she's initiated any individual conversation with me and I can't help but be a little surprised. My pause must have confused her and her face is closing up, as if she's embarrassed to have bothered me.

"Oh, sorr-..." she starts and turns away.

On instinct I reach out and grab her gently around the wrist. She doesn't shake me off. "No. Sorry, I was just daydreaming. Of course, we can talk." I lead her over to a quiet corner of the room, away from the guys chatting in the living area. "What can I help you with?"

She looks up at me, and for the first time in weeks, I'm staring down into her eyes again. Their oak brown depths are endless and in seconds I'm already getting lost in them.

"I have something for you," she says and I notice her holding a flat brown paper bag.

"Oh. What is it?" I can't guess what it might be, and I can't think of any reason she'd be giving me something.

"It's, ah, it's actually, from me and the kids in the orchestra. Um, kinda like, ah, an early thank you."

I'm shocked. I don't know what she's told them, but I'm surprised that she's told them anything at all. I guess she has no doubt that I'll follow through with my promise. I can't believe the confidence she has in me if that's the case.

"A thank you? For what?"

She doesn't smile, but something flickers in her eyes that fills me with warmth. A look of deep appreciation. One I can't imagine that I deserve.

"For giving us hope."

"Cadence..." What is it about this woman that touches the very core of me?

"I haven't promised them anything yet, I just told them, it's possible that someone may be answering our prayers."

I lean in, wanting her to hear every word, "You know I have no intention of ever breaking the deal we've made, right? You can count on that money."

"I know." And I hear it in her voice, she really does.

"Good." I smile. "Now, are you actually going to give me my gift?"

She laughs and it's like a fucking nightingale singing, and hands the small bag to me. "We've been practicing this over the last few days. The kids came in early to record it this morning. Sorry about the blurry video, we just did it on my iPhone."

"What's it of?" I open it and see a DVD. I'm burning with curiosity.

"You'll see. Or hear. We hope you like it. I chose it specifically for you. I hope you're not disappointed for believing in us." And then, she leans in, and grazes my cheek with her lips. "You're a really good guy, Sebastian."

I'm frozen to the spot. I'm torn between wanting to run to my laptop and put the DVD in, and pulling her back for another kiss.

She makes the decision for me.

"I'll see you guys tomorrow! Great rehearsal today!" she calls across the room as she walks away from me, lingering at the door for a moment for one last look, and then closing the door behind her.

"Hey! What's that?" Jez comes over to me, and takes the disc from my hands.

"Oi! Give it back. It's private."

"Oooh, private with our Cadey. We want to know!" Marius pipes up and jumps on the couch.

"Jez, give it the fuck back. It's none of your business!"

"Come and get it, piss ant!"

I pretend to give up and just as he turns away, I run over, leaping over the couch, and wrestle him to the floor. He grunts and tries to knee me in the groin as I straddle over him. He throws the DVD over to Marius before I can grab it from him. I punch him in the shoulder and he grabs my hand and twists it.

"Ah fuck!!! Let go, dickhead!" I scream, which just makes him twist harder. I manage to get my other arm free and give him a right hook to the left cheek.

"Motherfucker!" he grunts in pain, loosening his grip for a moment given me a chance to grab his throat with my hand.

"WHAT DO YOU PICKLEDICKS THINK YOU ARE DOING?!" Dennis' voice booms over us and we stop wrestling, still holding each other tight, but turn so we're both on our backs looking up at his face, so red it looks like it might just pop off his neck in a cloud of steam.

"Erm. He started it!" Jez nods to me.

"Did fucking not." I pout and tighten my grip around his neck and he pretends to choke.

"You have got to be fucking kidding me. Do you KNOW how much I pay in insurance for those girly hands of yours? And hire people to do everything from your laundry to your dishes to practically tying your shoelaces, for fuck's sake? It's so you don't hurt them doing anything more strenuous that jerking off. NOW FUCKING LET GO OF EACH OTHER!"

"Count to three and we'll do it at the same time," Jez tells him.

"Good lord, I should just let you kill yourselves and take the life insurance and go live on an island where I never have to listen to any string instruments ever again." He moans and presses the ball of his hand against his temple.

"You better do it or else they'll still be there in a week's time. Remember that time Jez didn't change his shirt for two weeks because no one laughed at the joke printed on it?" Brad reminds him.

"Oh, yeah! That was a good one! Hey, Dennis, knock knock."

"I'll knock knock your fucking heads together! Fucking hell. On three, okay, willywankers? One, two, three."

"Ooooof!" We let go and push each other away, biting back smiles.

"Guys, shut up and look at this." Marius waves to the laptop screen. He's put in the DVD.

We go over to the couch just as the video focuses.

It's Cadence. She's dressed as she was at rehearsal today. A long, sleek, sleeveless V-neck black dress and black ankle boots. She comes to the front of the lens. The camera shakes a bit and she laughs and reaches out, stabilizing it. Then without a word, she goes and sits down at the baby grand piano, where I first heard her play.

The cameraman walks over to her and zooms in on her face. She closes her eyes and places her hands on the keys. Taking a deep breath, she opens her eyes, and starts to play.

It's a beautiful melody that I think is from the soundtrack of *The Truman Show*. I don't know if there's any meaning behind her choosing this song, but it's a simple, gorgeous piece that sounds angelic coming from her talented fingers. Everyone is just as mesmerized as I am. It's hard to focus too much on each other during our rehearsals because to some extent we're all trying to work on our own parts, but here, unencumbered by our own need for perfection, we can really sit back and enjoy her performance.

Then, as the piece comes to a soft, gentle end, the camera zooms out and the rest of the room comes into view. Her entire orchestra is sitting there, instruments in hand and without missing a beat, as soon as she plays her last note, the orchestra lifts into song.

Cadence runs from the piano to the middle of the room and climbs onto her conductor's box, arms lifting, fingers alive, already directing her band to create their best sound.

Marius whoops when he realizes they're playing "The Fight Song" by Rachel Platten and holds up his fists and punches in time to the music.

They are good. Really good. Cohesive as an ensemble as well as individually talented. I watch them watching her, their passion matching hers look for look, note for note. There's a look of pride on her face that is infectious, and I wonder how it is I already feel a sense of belonging to this band, as if their future successes will be mine as well.

Just as the chorus breaks, on screen, a teenager drops his bow and stands up in his spot, holding up a sign with the lyrics.

We can't help but sing along at the top of our voices, grinning at each other during the impromptu karaoke session.

The song soon comes to an epic, overwhelming close. The entire orchestra all get to their feet and yell out, "THANK YOU, SEBASTIAN."

Cadence turns and gives the camera a small nod and smile and it fades to black.

I wonder how I can be physically rooted to this very spot and yet be moved solar systems emotionally.

"Dude, that was cool. What was it?" Jez asks me, gesturing to the blank laptop screen.

"It was, um, it was Cadence's school orchestra. She just, um, she wanted to show me something they were working on."

"Why'd they say 'thank you, Sebastian'?"

I don't want to tell them. I want it to be just between her and me. Well, and Marius and the kids. But not the rest of the guys.

Marius, in one of his rare insightful moments, sees me hesitating, interrupts and quickly changes the subject. "Oi, Brad, you know a lot about jockstrap itch. Does mine smell a little funky to you? Come have a sniff!" And as if he's a magician, pulls a pair of boxers out of his pocket.

Everyone, including me, groans, and just like that, it's forgotten.

I catch Marius' eye and give him a thankful look. He just winks and then turns back to chasing Brad around the room waving his underwear over his head. Ejecting the DVD from the laptop, I hold it against my chest for a moment before slipping it into my bag and trying to ignore the worried look that Dennis is giving me.

Chapter Thirteen

CADENCE

Another week has passed and I feel like the time is rushing past faster and faster by the day. There are about four more weeks of rehearsals scheduled before the band goes into the studio to record the pieces we've been working on. There are four pieces with piano which shouldn't take more than two or three recording sessions. The guys are worse perfectionists than I am though, so who knows how many takes it could take? But I don't care. The whole process is so much fun. I'm already starting to wonder if I should be pursuing some more recording work after my time with the Rock Chamber Boys.

After giving Sebastian the DVD last week, things have returned somewhat to normal between us. He must've shown the guys though, because they've all come up individually to me to congratulate me on doing a good job with the school orchestra. Truth is, I was so worried giving it to Sebastian. He leads this groundbreaking, award-winning string group, it was hard imagining how my amateur school orchestra would look to him. But I wanted him to know…that it wasn't just me, the kids appreciated it so much as well, and that it really wasn't for me, it was all for them.

Sometimes, in those quiet moments during our breaks, I sit and watch him, and I wonder, was I really wrong to end things with him before anything could start? Was I really afraid he was going to turn out like the men in my past? Had he ever done anything to indicate that? Other than the misunderstanding with Dennis' daughter, he hadn't done anything to show he was the rockstar player that I was so afraid he was going to be.

But then he'll shoot me a smile and my heart will float and sink in equal measure. And if a smile can affect me like that, how would I handle it when I was all in, and he was ready to be all out at any time? And he would. That's just been my luck. With my heart smashed to smithereens and me on my hands and knees trying to gather up the pieces. And some would inevitably be washed away in the torrent of tears.

So, yes. I was right.

It was just a case of reminding myself of that.

Like right now.

He's sitting in front of the window, cello in hand as he strums a quiet little melody, providing his own soundtrack to the darkening city skyline. I just want to come up behind him, run my hands up under his shirt and over the taut skin of his abdomen, and lay my face against his back. He's made me miss that intimacy. He's made me crave it. Crave it from him.

"Guys," Dennis says, walking into the middle of the room, and waving them all over.

I see Brad glance over at Sebastian who just shrugs.

"My friend Patrick owns a little live music club just a few streets from here and he's wondering if we want to play a small impromptu set there tonight around 10:00. Club fits about 2,000 people, and it'll be early so it won't be too bad, we can try out some of the new stuff. You guys up for it?"

As usual, they defer to Sebastian, and he just shrugs again, "Yeah, sure, why not. We'll chuck it up on twitter and FB, get some of our regulars out."

Dennis grins and admits, "Yeah, already did it," and runs out of the room before they can respond.

"Fucking hell, we should've just changed the name to "Dennis' hand puppets." Jez grumbles.

"No, thanks, I don't want the image of Dennis' hand up my ass out there in the public subconscious." Marius shudders.

"Guess we should all get some rest then, cut the rehearsal here. Is that all right, Cadence?" Jez asks me thoughtfully.

"Please, MIND an early minute? You HAVE been out of school for a long time." I grin and quickly pack up my stuff and leave the guys to it.

Just as I get into the car my phone beeps and I reach for it.

"You're coming tonight, right?" the text reads.

I don't recognize the number and text back. *"??"*

"It's Seb, Mary. How many other guys are you meant to be meeting tonight?"

"I didn't even have plans on meeting one."

"Ow"

"What? Did Marius' bow poke up your bum?" I tease him.

"No, your words. They hurt."

"Good."

Something about texting makes it easier to say these things to him. It feels good to joke around with him freely, like in those conversations when we first met.

"So, tonight?"

"What about it?"

"You wouldn't leave us hanging. What if no one shows up?"

"Then I'll never let you hear the end of it."

"But you gotta be there to witness our failure."

The phone dings again before I can answer.

"Please"

And again.

"It won't be the same without you."

I can't help but press the phone to my chest for a moment. Touched by his words. I stop one step short of squealing like one of my teenage students.

"Fine. Can I bring Sarah?"

"That nutso, sure."

"Then okay. I'll be there."

"I'll be waiting. See you soon, Mary."

This time I don't bite back the little squeal.

***

"Fuck, they are good." Sarah turns to me, and we're both sweating in this overheated club and from dancing to the band. The guys have just finished a forty-minute set, ending on a roof-raising version of AD/DC's "TNT". Patrick, the club owner, has saved us two booths on the side and we're waiting for the band to join us.

"I'm just going to go to the little girls' room, do you want to come with me?" Sarah asks.

"No, I'll stay here with our stuff. You'll be okay?" Knowing full well in a club, it's not Sarah who needs to watch out.

"I'll be fine, won't be a bit. Order me another vodka tonic?"

I nod and watch as she walks through the crowd, always in awe of how confident she is. Maybe being loved unconditionally by an adoring husband gives you that confidence. And maybe having ex-lovers who are determined to destroy you leads people to be more like me. I shake my head to get rid of the dark thoughts and smile when I see Marius wave to me over the bobbing, dancing heads on the dance floor as the band makes it over to the booth.

"How were we?" he asks as soon as he slips into the booth next to me.

"How were you what?" I pretend not to understand.

"The show!" He glares at me.

"Oh! I don't know, I took a nap..." I make a nonchalant face.

"Bitch!" Marius pinches my arm and I grin at him. "Where's your friend?"

"She's gone to the bathroom." I explain.

"And you didn't go with her?!? Don't you go in herds? Your girl membership card needs to be revoked!" Brad jokes.

I dip my fingers into my drink and flick them at the boys, who howl in protest.

Sebastian slides into the empty spot next to me, and leans in, yelling to be heard over the music. "How we were really?"

Even over the din I can hear the genuine interest in my opinion in his voice. "You guys were great. Really solid. The new stuff is dynamite," I smile at him.

"You should come up with us next time," he says seriously.

"It's the Rock Chamber BOYS, not Rock Chamber Boys and random music school teacher." I remind him.

"You know we see you as every bit a part of the band that we are." He insists.

"But I'm not."

"Maybe you should be." He shrugs when I question him with my look.

"That would cramp your style." Your rockstar, groupies in every port lifestyle, I think to myself.

"I'd make room for you, Cadence." He says earnestly. And it takes everything I have not to believe him.

"Cadey! Move over!" Sarah's voice pulls us apart and Sebastian moves over to make room for her.

"Hey, how come SHE gets to call you Cadey?" Marius asks.

"She doesn't 'get to', she's just not as scared of me as you guys are," I grin at him and he pouts.

"What'll you guys have?" Patrick comes over with a waitress and takes the guys' drinks order.

Sarah nudges me and whispers into my ear, "Ugh, there's some slut in the bathroom talking about how she's slept with half the band and she's going for Sebastian tonight."

I feel as if a frozen icicle's stabbed me in the stomach but try to pass it off as nothing. "Yeah, um, I guess they get that a lot."

"Hey guys! You were so great!"

I look up and see Hailey and a tall leggy blonde coming towards us. She waves to me and I smile back. We've seen a lot of each other in the last few weeks as she comes in and out during rehearsals helping Dennis out with some admin work and odd jobs for the band. They really do treat her like a little sister and she's been nothing but sweet to me.

"Hey, Hailey, this is my friend, Sarah." I introduce her to my friend.

Hailey waves to Sarah who outright ignores her. I nudge her, surprised at her behavior, and she rolls her eyes and raises her hand in a halfhearted wave back to Hailey.

"What's wrong with you?" I turn to my friend.

"That's the girl from the bathroom," she growls.

"Hailey's friend? I've never met her before."

"No, Hailey. She's the one who was talking about scoring with Sebastian tonight." Sarah scrunches her face up, unimpressed.

"No, you mean her friend, the leggy blonde. Hailey's the one who waved to you, she's the one we saw with Sebastian that night after the concert."

"Babe, I know exactly which one it is. I'm telling you it was her," she insists.

"Did you SEE her say it?" I need to know for sure.

"I was in the stall but I could see through the crack, I promise you it's her."

"Whatever, it doesn't matter." I wave her off, not wanting to hear any more. But it does.

I can't help but notice when Hailey comes over and slides in between Sebastian and Jez, laughing with them over some inside joke, and they're tickling her and she's obviously enjoying every moment.

I know I don't have any right to care, having refused any attempt by Sebastian to start something between us, but I can't help but remember that shock of seeing her with him that night, and the crushing feeling of hurt and disappointment. No matter Sebastian's explanations about what happened and what she means to him, which now seems as though it's not completely true anyway.

Sarah growls next to me, and I look over at her and she gestures with her head to Hailey and Sebastian again, their heads together as she's showing him something on her phone, her hand on his leg. My heart twists in my chest and I can't help but curse my own weakness, stopping me from being with him.

"Come on, screw this shit, let's go have some fun, babe." Sarah grabs my hand, forcing me to look away from the torturous scene playing out in front of me and drags me out to the dance floor.

I see Marius and Brad follow us and I turn and wait for them, pretending to look at my watch to get them to hurry up. Brad laughs and grabs my hand and the four of us push our way into the middle of the crowd.

Patrick booked an eighties cover band for after the Rock Chamber Boys set and the clubgoers are eating it up. It doesn't take long for us to be completely lost in the nostalgic familiarity of the songs, singing along to Toni Basil's "Oh Mickey!" and bumping and grinding next to strangers, laughing as we mix up the words.

I'm losing myself in the music and the fun that Brad, Marius, Sarah and I are having, and best of all, forgetting about the scenes of Hailey seducing Sebastian back at the booth. The crowd around us builds as people start to recognize them from their performance and hordes of women start to gather around Marius and Brad, who are lapping up the attention, but making sure Sarah and I are never too far away.

Suddenly, I feel a hand on my shoulder, gently nudging me to the side, Sebastian and Hailey have joined us and the others are making room for them to join the dance circle. In the corner of my eye I can see Sarah glare at the two of them, and she turns to dance with a bachelorette party to the side of us. Hailey's hand is gripping Sebastian's shoulder, as if afraid to let him go. Even when he leans into whisper to me, "You having a good time?" I see her tugging on his shoulder and away from me.

The best way to not respond in a way that will cause me regret, I decide, is just to ignore them altogether. I turn my back to Sebastian in the guise of dancing with Marius. I lean over and make a joke about how the Rock Chamber Boys should do an '80s retrospective some time and he laughs, taking my hand and twirling me around. Mid twirl, I catch Sebastian's eye for a moment, and he looks hurt, but only for a second before I notice his arms around Hailey's waist and she's dropping her head onto his shoulder.

I twirl back to face Marius and feel a body up against me.

Sebastian.

I close my eyes telling myself, it's okay to enjoy his touch for just a moment. I've been so good for so long, despite craving him with every fiber of my being. I lean back and reach behind me to touch his arm.

It's not him. It's not Sebastian's arm. It's too rough.

I look up and Marius is standing in front of me, so I know it's not him either. Two hot hands then grab me from behind around the hips and pull me back, banging hard against the stranger's chest. I try to turn, but the hands are holding me tight and I can feel the body start to grind against me. I feel repulsed by this uninvited assault. I start to struggle, but the hands around my hips grip me harder, almost bruising me to keep me in place.

"Get off me!" I yell, and kick my heel up behind me, trying to aim for the grabber's shins.

Marius comes forward, his face angry and he tries to reach for the person holding onto me. I shake my head at him, not wanting him to get involved; I can take care of this dickhead myself. He stands back but keeps watching close so I know I won't get into too much trouble. I struggle harder, lifting my leg and stomp down hard on the guy's foot. He roars and doesn't let go but loosens his grip. I manage to shake him off and turn around. I see him for the first time, it's a drunk guy that had been hanging around us since we'd gotten to the dance floor. His face is red and he lurches towards me again.

"I said, get the FUCK off me, ASSHOLE!" I scream in his face pushing him away. I turn back to Marius who's now been joined by Brad but before any of us can react, he yanks me back by my hair, and lifts his other hand and slaps me hard across the face. The strike is so hard, it blinds me, and I'm flung to the side, twisting my wrists as I try to break my fall while crumpling to the floor.

"Fucking, cockteasing slut." He slurs and I feel his rank breath on me as he reaches for me again, leaning over me as he wraps his hand in my hair, pulling me to my feet.

"Oh my god! Cadence!" I hear Sarah yell over the music and thumping in my head.

And then, I fall to the floor again as the guy is yanked away and forced to let me go.

"Brad! Marius! No!" I hear a voice, I think it's Hailey's but I'm not sure as I feel someone scoop me up.

This time it really is Sebastian.

Even in my haze I curse myself, how could I have not felt this difference?

"It's okay, Mary..." Sebastian whispers to me and the use of my nickname causes the tears to instantly spring from my eyes. My head pounds so hard I can't help but let it fall against his chest. I let out an involuntary sob as there's a streak of pain across the side of my head.

"Shhh, baby girl, I've got you. You're okay, I've got you. No one's going to get to you now." His voice soothes me, and I let myself grow limp in his arms. Even through the pain, I feel safe and warm.

"Sebastian," I moan softly, wanting him to know I know it's him.

"Shhh. I'm here. Don't you worry about a thing," he soothes me even as I feel his chest rise and fall, and his breath hiss from the effort of carrying me and pushing through the crowds to take me to safety. I don't know how he does it, move all the people out the way, but he never stops, not for a moment. And in that moment, I have no doubt that he would part the stars to make a path to safety for me if he had to.

"Over here, Sebastian," I vaguely hear Sarah's voice and I can just make out that we're now leaving the club. The sounds are fading away, and I can hear his heart thump hard against my own pulsing temple. One beat for every two of his. That's no surprise, he has twice as much heart as me. I try to smile up at him, but his face is serious, set on just getting me out of there.

"Open the door, Hank," I feel Sebastian's voice rumble through his torso. There's the sound of the car door opening, and then he lays me gently down in the back seat. Taking his jacket off, he drapes it over me, and I feel his cool hand touch me gently on my burning cheek. "God, Mary..." he sighs.

I try to sit up, to see him more clearly...to thank him but he presses gently yet firmly on my shoulder, keeping me down. "Don't sit up, just lay there, we got you."

Someone slides in from the other door, it must be Sarah, then the doors slam shut and it's quiet. I try to look around but I can't see him.

Then, from the other side of the door, the voices are muted but I can just make out him saying, "Take them back to the hotel, Hank. Go in the back way and tell Mark not to let anyone but Dennis and the band onto our hotel room floor."

Hank mumbles something and as he gets in the car, Sebastian finishes with, "We'll be back later. Don't worry about us. Take care of them."

The car starts and drives away. Hot tears drip down my cheeks, burning my eyes, and I can just make out his blurry image through the window.

"Sebastian..." I say, trying to reach out for him and then everything fades to black.

Chapter Fourteen

SEBASTIAN

The moonlight bathes the room in a soft cool white glaze. As the silvery orb rises higher and higher in the night sky, I watch the shadows cast on Cadence's face change. The soft light catches on the bridge of her nose, on her flickering eyelashes, on the curve of her lips; showing me a hundred and one different faces to her. Each one twisting tighter and tighter.

Even in the dark I can see the bruise spread further and further across her cheek and over her eye as each minute ticks by. Dark and purple, there are spidery veins running like streams over the expanse of the wound. I lean in and press the cold compress against her forehead, willing the soft, damp fabric to soak up the pain and leave her the delicate, pristine Cadence that I know.

Sarah told me that Cadence passed out for a while on the drive home, but was up and alert by the time the doctor had come to see her. They'd given her a painkiller and she'd fallen asleep by the time I'd arrived at my hotel room.

Sarah wouldn't leave without her friend, so Marius offered to bunk with Brad for the night so she could sleep in his room that adjoins with mine.

And here I am, wondering how I could have let this happen. How, even in my presence, watching over her, Cadence is now lying in my bed, with the side of her face brutalized under the hand of a drunken idiot.

It had all happened so fast. And it was not the way tonight was supposed to end.

I had been on such a high performing tonight. It'd been the first time I'd been on stage performing since we had really gotten to know her. As with the first concert, I couldn't keep my eyes off Cadence in the audience during the whole set. I drank it all in, the way her face lit up in those first few bars of each song, trying to figure out what we were going to play. And then the way she would lose herself in the music, dancing to the rhythm of my cello.

I couldn't wait to get back to her in that booth. I hadn't wasted any time pressing up against her, our heads leaning in so we could hear one other, I'd believed everything I'd said to her. These last few weeks, I'd felt like she was part of the band, and if there was the tiniest inkling of her thinking she would join, I'd fight to the death for her right to become one of us. She's more than proven she can keep up with us, and she has the creativity and talent to only make us better.

But when she left the booth with Brad and Marius and I watched her dancing with them I felt a lightning strike of jealousy rip through me, something I'd never felt before. After a few songs of absolute torture, I grabbed Hailey and dragged her to the dance floor with me, wanting just to be near Cadence. But she turned away from me each chance she got. It made me really wonder, is there something going on with her and Marius? Since the day he drove her home, there's seemed to be a closeness between the two of them, and she jokes with him and flirts with him when she's always careful to keep me at arm's length.

At least I could understand when it was with Brad and Marius, but then when the fuckhead came up behind her, it almost killed me to watch her lean back into him, letting him grind against her and her reaching up to touch him. Hailey had watched me seethe and held me back, telling me I had to let her do what she wanted.

But then, when it seemed like she didn't want his advances anymore, and was trying to get away, I couldn't get to her fast enough. We'd drifted a little way from the group and hordes of people were in the way when I tried to get to her. I keep playing that image in my head of him yanking her by the hair back and striking her across the face with his backhand. In that moment I could've died. Or sold my soul to the devil to let me relive that moment, only this time, I would have gotten to her in time.

She had been so limp in my arms, so small and helpless. I wanted to breathe life back into her, back into the woman I first met in the shop, ranting and lecturing me, the woman in the music class room, her face lit up with pride, the woman in rehearsals, lost in the passion of creating music - not this battered, injured little bird in my arms.

When I went back to the club, the guys had dragged the asshole out to the side alley and were teaching him what happens when you hit women.

Marius held him back while Brad was letting out some repressed anger. When they saw me, they'd each taken an arm and waited. Watched me take my belt off and wrap one end around my hand. They knew what was coming, and there wasn't an ounce of mercy for anyone who got what they deserved if I'd decided they deserved it.

"Do you think hitting a woman who doesn't want your sticky, dirty fingers on her makes you a big man?" I'd come up close to his face, and asked him; his stinking breath making me disgust with him even more.

He'd just whimpered.

"Well, it's not. It makes you a small, small man. A small tiny man with a teeny weeny, shriveled chicken dick. One that's going to shrink up into your body and take a long, long time before it's going to want to come back out again, when I'm done with you."

I'd raised my hand over my head.

"Sebastian. Don't."

A voice had spoken up.

It was Dennis.

"She wouldn't want this."

"She didn't want him either, and look what happened," I turned around and reminded my manager.

"So, how does that make you better than him?"

I replayed the moment his hand had hit her and the way she'd crumpled to the floor. And I wanted to hurt him, have him crumple to the floor as many times as it'd take for me to forget that moment.

But it wouldn't ever be enough.

"Let him go, guys." Dennis had said to them. And they'd hesitated.

"Tell 'em, Sebastian." It took a moment, but I'd lowered my hand and nodded.

He'd fallen to the ground, sniveling, hugging his side from the gifts Brad had lain on his body.

"Come on," Dennis' hand was warm and firm on my shoulder and he'd led me away.

And now we were here.

Me watching over her and wondering if I was ever going to get over the guilt.

***

"Sebastian?" A soft voice speaks my name and I lift my head from the side of the bed. Her eyes are opening slowly and she tries to move.

"Hey, you...don't move. Can I get you something?"

She clears her throat gently, "I'm a little thirsty. Where am I?"

"You're in my bed."

"Oh. Well, was it as good for me as it was for you?"

I sigh softly and smile, glad to see some of her spark back. "It's always good for me, Cadey, even the times it's so good you can't remember them." I get up from the chair by the bed and she makes a soft noise. "What's wrong?" I turn back to her.

"Um, nothing, just...um...don't leave," she says in a small voice, as if embarrassed.

"I'm just going to get you some water...then I'll be right back. okay?"

"Ok," she says softly and I squeeze her hand to reassure her.

I grab a bottle of water and a straw from the drinks cart and come back to the bedroom.

Her breathing is soft and steady again, and I guess she's fallen back asleep. I tiptoe out only to hear her call out to me.

"I'm not asleep, don't leave, please."

Her vulnerability breaks my heart. How could anyone do this to her?

"Hey, don't worry, I'm right here." I sit back down and hold the bottle for her to take a drink. She takes a small sip and lies back, as if exhausted by the effort.

"Seb?" It's the first time she's ever called me by my shortened name.

"Yeah?"

"Can you...can you play something for me?" she asks me shyly.

Oh my god. Yes, sweet angel. "Oh, of course, why?"

"It, um, it just comforts me."

"Sure, anything in particular?"

"No, you pick. You'll know what I want better than I do."

I grab my cello and sit back down. She smiles at me and then closes her eyes, settling down deep into my bed.

I pull the bow across the strings, my hands already knowing what I want to play.

"How 'bout this one?" I play each note slowly and deliberately, letting each sound linger in the air and soak into her bruises and wash the hurt away. She smiles and nods, eyes still closed. Halfway through the song she opens her eyes and watches me. In the soft glow of the late night, with her watching me, my fingers find their own way on the strings as I smile at her and mouth the words, "I'll stand by you, I'll stand by you, won't let nobody hurt you..."

She sighs gently as the song comes to an end. "Thank you."

I just nod and start to play a soft melody I'd been playing with for the last few weeks.

"What's this one called? It's so pretty. Is it an original?"

"Yes. It doesn't have a name yet," I lie to her.

"Let's give it one."

"Ok. What do you think it should be?"

"Something beautiful."

"That's easy. I have an idea."

"Ok good. You can tell me when I wake up," she starts to slur and her eyes close as her breathing slows.

"Ok..."

"Just don't stop playing."

"I won't."

And I play until she falls asleep, the sun comes up and my fingers bleed.

CADENCE

"So, then Sebastian put you into the car and you passed out! You don't remember that part?" Sarah asks as she fluffs the pillows behind me and pushes me back to lie against them.

"Well, not really. I remember the guy, and then I remember the doctor and then the Sebastian part last night."

"What do you mean the Sebastian part last night?"

"Um, nothing. Where is everyone?" I look around. It's deathly quiet, which is rare whenever the band is around.

"Well, the guys are outside wanting to come visit and Dennis is off dealing with …well, let's just say, there were some photos."

"Of what?"

"Of Sebastian bashing up the guy."

"What?" Oh, Sebastian.

"Don't worry about it, Dennis is dealing with it." She waves her hand, trying to get me to stop asking.

"Damn."

"Can I let the guys in?" She asks when we hear a soft knock on the door.

"Sure. Wait, how do I look?"

"Like you ran into a telephone pole with your face over and over again for fun."

"Nice." To be honest, it was how I felt.

"Guys, come in," Sarah calls out to the guys.

The door opens slowly and Brad, Marius and Jez file in, tiptoeing in one by one and standing in the far corner of the room. They look sheepish and don't say anything and avoid any eye contact.

"Hey, guys," I say to them. And they just lift their hands and do small finger wave. It's kinda weird.

"Um, how are you guys?" I ask, looking at Sarah, who just shrugs.

They look at each other and say nothing. Finally, Brad elbows Jez and he takes a small step forward.

"We are fine, thank you, how are you?" Jez finally whispers, enunciating each word slowly, before taking a step back to lean against the wall.

I blink.

Someone has replaced the band with some sort of pod people.

"Um, guys, what's going on?" I ask them again.

They bite their lips and look at each other again. This time it's Brad that gets the elbow and he leans forward.

"Sebastian said we're not allowed to make any noise or bother you," Brad whispers even lower than Jez did. "He said if we did, he'd cut our tongues off, since we didn't need them because we are an instrumental band."

I can't help but laugh and then flinch as a sharp pain torches its way through my head.

"Owww." I moan and hold the side of my head with my hand.

"Uh oh." Marius' eyes bug out and he presses his finger against his lips.

I giggle and wave him forward, he looks around before approaching the bed and leans in to look at me right in the eye.

"Guys, stop, I'm fine." I say, smiling and pinching Marius' cheek. "You can talk normally."

"But Sebastian said…"

"Is Sebastian here right now?" I ask, both as a way of making my point, and trying to find out where he is.

They shake their head in unison like a row of the clown heads game at the county fair.

"So, it'll just be between you and me." I wink at them.

"And Sarah?" The guys look over at her.

"Yeah, you in, Sarah?" I ask her, grinning.

"Dude, anything to stop them tiptoeing around and trying to mime shit. It's been a weird hour with them out there like Cirque du Soleil clown freaks." She throws her hands up, exasperated.

"So, please be normal now." I beg them.

They look at each other for a moment, and then sigh, as if they've been holding their breath for an hour.

"We were so worried about you!" Marius sits down on the bed, and reaches over and grabs a chocolate from the box Sarah brought with her.

"No need, guys. I really am fine." I'm touched at how genuinely worried they seem.

"We're so sorry we didn't deck that guy before he got to you." Brad hangs his head, and as bad as I feel, I guess it's nothing compared to having had to watch it and feel helpless. But it wasn't their fault. I had wanted to take care of it myself, I didn't think the guy would actually get so violent. I reach over and pat Marius on the shoulder, his face is red and I feel bad that I'd put them through it.

"So where is Dennis now?" I ask, wanting to get more information on the photos supposedly leaked about Sebastian.

"Er…"

"What?" This can't be good.

"Sebastian said…"

"Guys, fuck Sebastian… he's not here. Tell me what's going on?" The pounding behind my eye is getting worse and I want to hear what they have to say before I take another painkiller and it makes me woozy.

"Look, nothing actually happened, it just looks bad."

"What looks bad?"

"Tell her. She'll find out eventually, and she's getting worked up," Sarah suggests.

Jez sighs and Brad nods, encouraging him to talk.

"Look, after Sebastian grabbed you and took you out to the car, um, Brad and Marius grabbed that asshole and dragged him outside, um, you know, to teach him a lesson."

"Oh guys…" I look over at them and they look sheepish.

"So, then Sebastian shows up and, um, well, let's say, he was pissed."

"What did he do?"

"He didn't do anything."

"Guys, come on."

"Look he didn't, he, um, he just threatened the guy, er, with his belt, but he didn't actually do anything. Dennis got there and talked him out of it. Which, frankly, I'm surprised worked. He was really fucking pissed."

"But, well, the guy's friends had followed us out there and took photos of Seb with the belt in his hand and um, threatening him."

"Damn. Idiot!" I did not want this. I hate that I have put the guys in any sort of PR trouble. It's part of the reason I didn't want to get involved with Sebastian in the first place.

"He didn't do anything to the guy, Cadence. He...might've, but he didn't. These claims are bogus. Don't worry about it. Dennis will take care of it. He knows what he's doing."

"Where is Sebastian now?" I ask, wondering if he's trying to stay away from me, the troublemaker.

"We don't know." Brad shrugs.

"He'll come back. He has loner tendencies, he just needs time to work through shit." Jez reaches over and squeezes my arm to reassure me.

"Now...YOU guys," I point to Brad and Marius, ready to lecture them for their part in this.

"Uh oh....nap time!" And they run out of the room.

SEBASTIAN

I hear the guys come back to the rehearsal room from visiting Cadence in my room. I'm dying to ask them how she is, but I don't want to hear the same lecture they've been giving me for the last few hours.

"Hey," Jez comes to sit down next to me.

"Hey." I say, not looking up from my phone.

"She's okay." He tells me, knowing me well enough to know I'm dying to know but too stubborn to ask.

"Good. Yeah, um, good to hear."

"She's asking after you."

"Yeah, I'll, um, I'll go visit her later, she needs her rest. You guys probably got her all riled up."

"We didn't," he protests instantly, and I feel bad for saying it. I know they care about her a lot. "Anyway, she's fine, maybe a little rattled, but her bruise doesn't look too bad." He adds, running his fingers along the side of his face as if picturing her.

I grip my phone tight, wondering how he could be so blasé about her injuries.

"Yo, Seb. Why don't you get off your ass and stop being a dick and go visit your girl?" Brad yells over to me from his spot in front of the TV.

"She's not my girl," I reply through gritted teeth.

"Coulda fooled me," Marius says under his breath.

"What did you say?" I challenge him.

Marius stands up and faces me, "Come on, man. You think we don't know what's going on? What's been going on since you brought her here? You're so fucking in love with her, you can't see straight. Although, since I'm guessing you haven't gotten her into bed yet, I'm surprised you can walk straight too."

"Marius..." Jez says, in a warning tone, and stands up, moving in between us.

"No. He needs to hear this. She is lying in a strange bed over there, probably scared out of her fucking mind, not to mention hurt, and he's just sitting here because what? Actually, I don't know why? Why don't you tell us?"

"Shut up, Marius," I snap at him, my fists gripping the sides of my legs, holding my anger back.

"No, I'm not going to fucking shut up."

"Hey, maybe you're the one who's so in love with her." I throw the accusation at him, glad to finally get it off my chest.

Marius snickers, and waves his hand dismissing my words. "Yeah, keep deflecting."

"You're the one who flirts with her, dances with her. Hey, she might not even have been on the dance floor if it wasn't for you." The comment hit below the belt, but it's too late for me to take it back.

He looks at me hurt for a moment, and I want to apologize, but I can't. I need to blame someone for what happened to her.

"You are such an asshole. Don't blame what happened on me."

"You were right there! Why didn't you stop it?!" I spring up onto my feet and hurl my words at him.

"She didn't want me to." His voice somehow still remains calm, which just enrages me further.

"Who cares? Get the girl OUT of the dangerous situation!"

I've pushed too far.

"I told you, she didn't want me to!" He growls and his face twists into a red rage, throwing his arms over his head.

"You do it anyway."

"So how does that make me different than the guy who's grabbing her?"

"It's for her own good. She got hurt."

"You don't think I feel bad about that? She's like a little sister to me, man. You think I don't feel like shit that I was right there and didn't stop it?"

For the first time since it happened, I see the guilt painted all over his face. It's how I feel inside and it's horrifying to see it I've made him feel it too.

Before I can say anything, Dennis walks through the door.

He knows us well enough to know there's something going on, but he ignores it.

"It's taken care of," he says, referring to the photos, I assume.

"And?" I ask as I watch him walk to the drinks cart. He's obviously had a long day.

"And that's it. It's done."

"How much?" Brad wants to know. It's not the first time Dennis has had to buy us out of some bad publicity. It's just part of our life now.

"Enough."

We know better than to try to get more information from him. He downs his drink and sits down on the couch. Naturally, we gather around him.

"Are we going to have to talk about Cadence?" He turns to us, his tone serious.

"What do you mean?" Marius asks for clarification.

"You know what I mean. Four hotblooded males and one woman. It's my worst nightmare. It's been my worst nightmare since I took you guys on."

"You don't have anything to worry about." Marius responds.

"I'm not so sure about that." Dennis leans forward and peers at Marius, tilting his head.

"Well, don't look at me, I just told the guys, she's like a little sister to me." Marius points to me. "Ask him."

"Sebastian? Is this something we're going to have to sort out? Say it now before it's too late." Dennis

"No." I answer with one word, not trusting myself to not reveal my true feelings.

"Seb." Dennis says warningly.

"I said no."

"I've known you for ten years now. I know everything about you. I know what you smell like during every part of the day. I know that you like no sugars in your coffee in the morning and three at night. I've made it my business and YOUR business to know what you want even before you want it. So, I'm going to ask you one more time. Do I need to worry?"

"I said no." I take a breath, trying to keep my voice calm. "I've got it under control."

"I wish I could believe you, mate."

That makes two of us.

He's right. I had to sort this out, once and for all.

Chapter Fifteen

CADENCE

It's been three days since the incident at Patrick's club and I've pretty much seen nothing but the inside of my bedroom. After I left the hotel Sarah brought me home and won't leave my side. I had to get a doctor to come see me and tell her that I was okay to get back to my life.

A month ago I would've told you that laid up in bed for a half a week, what I'd miss most was my kids. But it turns out, all I could think about was the band and missing rehearsals. Missing the banter, missing the music, and yes, missing Sebastian.

What was I going to do when he wasn't going to be a part of my life anymore?

"Watcha thinkin' about?" Sarah asks me, her attention still on the road.

She's offered to take me to rehearsal, and I couldn't refuse, after everything she'd done for me.

"Um, nothing, just hoping I haven't become too rusty after no practice for the last few days."

"You'll be fine, honey, they'll understand."

"I know, but they shouldn't have to. I don't want to set them back because I haven't been up to it, this is serious stuff. It's just some fun for me, but they're big business. Big money."

"Don't we know it." Sarah winks at me, and I cringe a little inside. Now that I know the band and the kind of people and musicians they are…and how much fun I have spending time with them, I would've done all of it for the experience alone.

The money is the right thing for the school. I just wonder if it was the right thing for me.

***

"He's not here?" I ask when I get upstairs, not seeing Sebastian around.

"Um, no babe. No big deal, he, er, wasn't feeling real well this morning." Brad says, patting me gently on the arm.

"Is it because of me?" I ask, knowing the answer already.

"Wha? No! Jez's paranoia's rubbing off on you."

I know he's not telling the truth, but I'm not ready to make a thing of it yet. I scared him off. That night in his bedroom after the incident, I pushed him too far. He had to help me, he's too good to have just left, but I haven't seen him since. He just wants to make it clear that he's holding up his part of the bargain.

I can't complain, I'm the one who's held him at arm's length for a month. And now I'm getting what I wanted all along. And now suddenly five more weeks sounds like a sentence in hell.

***

"Miss Bray?" Jenny, the orchestra's first flute comes up to me after our weekly Friday rehearsal. A small, sweet Taiwanese girl, I've heard her speak maybe ten words all year. But I feel like I know her just as well as any of my kids. It's just all our communication is through the music. She wears her heart on every note she plays.

"Jenny, is everything all right?" I feel bad once I say it, not wanting to seem so alarmed that she's come to talk to me.

"Um, no, I don't want to bother you but...?"

"What's going on?"

"I don't think I can be part of the orchestra anymore."

I am momentarily shocked. She's been a part of the band for four years, since year eight and now, in her final year, she's thinking of leaving?

"But, why?"

She goes quiet, looking up at me, and I can see tears starting to fall.

I lay my hand gingerly on her shoulder and lead her to some chairs. She sits down and I reach over to squeeze her hand.

"You can talk to me."

"My parents just said I... I can't have flute lessons anymore, they say I have to get a job instead, and, and they're not going to be able to afford the cost to go to Nationals either. We, we just don't have the money." She says the last words and drops her head down, her hair falling to cover her face but I can still see it burn red with embarrassment.

"Oh, Jenny." I don't know what to say to her. I'm devastated for her. The problems with not being able to play flute is just part of it, I can't imagine the burden on such a young girl to have to worry about her family's financial problems.

I take a chance and reach out to hug her. She doesn't pull away. Her head is still dropped but I can feel sobs wrack through her body. I don't blame her, if I'd been told I couldn't play in the band any more I'd react much the same way.

"Hey, hey," I lift her chin up. "There's nothing that says you can't keep playing in the orchestra. We can work it out."

"We can't," she whimpers, looking at me her eyes sad and wet. "My parents were very clear. I either had to be at school or working. No time for music lessons or rehearsals. And no way to afford the fee for the trip to Nationals anyway, so what's the point in being in orchestra? Leave that spot for another student who can go, they said."

"Would you like me to talk to them? Maybe we can work something out, I'm happy for you to have a pulled back rehearsal schedule. You are so talented, it would be such a shame for you to miss it after all the work you've put in."

She just shakes her head and covers her face as her sobs grow louder. I know it's not just about the music but that the other parts of her life weighing on her as well. It's moments like this that make being a teacher, being so close to my students so hard. You can only help them so much.

"It's just so unfair," she whimpers softly and my heart breaks for her.

"Oh, Jenny," I stroke her hair gently, letting her have her safe space to let out her frustrations. I have to bite back my own tears. Their losses and disappointments are just as much mine as their wins and achievements.

"I'm so sorry, Miss Bray, I'm so sorry," she stands up suddenly, looking at me for a moment, then grabbing her bags and running out the door.

"Jenny!" I follow and call after her, but she's halfway down the hallway before I even get to the doorway.

"Goddammit!" I yell to the empty room, angry that I didn't get to help her at all.

I stand for a moment, and something breaks inside me. And the utter injustice of it all floods me.

"Fuckfuckfuckfuckfuck!" I grab a chair and slam it down on top of another, stacking them to tidy the room.

I can't help but let the tears fall. The poor girl. So, so talented, so very hard-working to get where she has with her music, and now, because of...what? money, she has to stop! I have no doubt about the family's financial difficulties, it's a common theme of all the kids in the school, being in a low-income district. But seeing the impact on the kids and the decisions they have to make, when they should be encouraged for every aspect of their future is so disheartening. And days like today make me wish I didn't have to see it.

"ARGHHHH!" I yell again, the scream helping to relieve the tension in my blood. I collapse onto my piano stool and sob, for a moment wishing I had the power to save the world.

"Cadence?"

I whip around, there shouldn't be anyone left at the school and I'm horrified that someone has heard me.

"Sebastian! What are you doing here?"

"Are you okay?" He takes a hesitant step into the classroom, and I wonder how much of my meltdown he witnessed.

I turn back to the piano and quickly try to wipe away the tears. How many times is he going to see me like this?

"Um, yeah, I'm a, I'm fine. What's going on?"

I turn back around and he's right there next to me, kneeling down next to the piano stool, staring me right in the eyes.

"Something's wrong, tell me. Is your...um, is your cheek hurting?" He reaches up, and with a feather-light touch, runs the back of his cool hand against my bruised cheek.

I close my eyes and enjoy the soothing feel of his cool skin against mine. It's the first time I've seen him since that night, almost a whole week. A whole week to process and obsess over what happened. Only to find that it doesn't matter what I tell myself, when he's here, in my presence, touching me, nothing else seems to matter.

"Cadence?" he whispers and my eyes flutter open.

"Um, no it's, it's not my cheek. I'm okay." I pull my face away, a little embarrassed that I succumb to his touch so easily.

"Then tell me."

"It's just something with one of my students." I stand up and walk away, trying to put some distance between us so I can think. "Wha- why are you here, Sebastian?"

"I just wanted to check that you're okay." He stands up, turning on his feet to follow me around the room.

"You could've checked while I was right there, lying in your bed. Or at the last two rehearsals that you missed." I say to the empty side of the room, wondering if he can hear the hurt in my voice.

"I know. I'm sorry. I just...I had to take care of something. I had to sort something out."

"Something...more important?"

His head whips around and he frowns.

"Something more important than you?" And then he mumbles something under his breath, and it sounds like, "If only there was such a thing."

"There is. The band." I remind him, "I know the band comes above all."

He doesn't answer and I know he knows it's true. And I'm not surprised, I'm not even hurt. Of course, it's the most important thing to him, definitely ranks higher than me, someone he's only known for a month.

"Not anymore."

And then, out of nowhere, he takes three steps to cross the room to stand in front of me. Dragging a long deep breath into his lungs, he slides his hands to up cradle the sides of my face, staring into my eyes for a moment before he leans down and presses his lips against mine.

Chapter Sixteen

SEBASTIAN

I'm kissing her. I'm finally fucking kissing her. And I don't think I can ever stop.

Her mouth, slightly opened in surprise from my unexpected kiss, is warm and soft against my lips. Her breath is sweet and doughy, like freshly baked bread. And that addicting scent of orange blossoms from her hair is awash over my face, and I'm trying to devour her, with kiss after kiss after kiss, my hands cradling the sides of her face.

I don't know what I expected when I took those steps across the classroom to her. Just that, it was time.

And now, her cheeks, so supple in my hands, and her hands gripping the sides of my head and tangled in my hair, I wonder how I've managed to restrain myself for so long. How we both have. I can taste her desire, she's been wanting this just as much as I have.

"Sebastian," she moans, as we pull apart for breath.

We stare at each other, panting. And then reach for each other again. As if pushed together by unseen hands that have long planned our fate and are frustrated by our folly in insisting on staying apart.

This time it's her lips that press, urgent, against mine, pushing them open, her tongue pushing deep into my mouth. A soft moan vibrates from the back of her throat when I slide my hands to run down her back and grip the fleshy cheeks of her ass, pulling her against me. Her body moves against me just as I've imagined it all these weeks, fitting in along the angles and curves of my own body.

She was made for me.

"Oh, god, Cadence," it's my time to moan. And she sighs in response.

And then suddenly the kiss is over.

She stiffens for a split second and pulls away from me, covering her lipstick-stained mouth in horror.

"Oh my god, no no no no no." She stares at me, with a look of regret in her eyes.

"Well, um, that's not quite the response I was hoping for," I say, blinking, still trying to figure out what's happening.

"We can't do this." She's still shaking her head. I'm almost afraid it'll shake her brain loose.

"Yes, we can. In fact, we just did," I remind her.

"No, I can't do this."

"Um, then who was I just kissing?"

"Sebastian!"

"Cadence, I'm serious. This dance we're doing, has got to stop. I'm going to put a stop to it."

"What?" She screeches, and I can't tell if it's out of fear or pent-up frustration.

I walk over to her and pull the envelope out of my pocket.

"This is for you."

"What is it?"

"Well, read it."

"It's...it's a $50,000 check."

"Well, it's a receipt. Yup."

"For $50,000."

"Yes."

"To me."

"Well, to the school. That's what this money was meant for, wasn't it?"

"Yes, but."

I press a finger to her lips.

"Just...just shush for a minute." And I move a finger to her temple, "And shush up here, too, and just listen to me, hear me out. And then decide."

She starts to say something, and then bites down on her tongue. And nods.

I lean over and press a gentle kiss to her lips and she sighs.

"You're no longer tied to me for any reason. And the money is no longer contingent on any contract. I wanted to donate this money to the school, and it's done. You couldn't send it back if you tried. So now...we're not bound by any contract. You don't have to play in the band if you don't want to, and I don't have to keep my hands off you to make you stay. We can make decisions based on what we should've done this whole fucking time."

"What's that?"

"What we want."

Her head whips up and her eyes lock on mine. I can see a sparkle coming to life deep in the deepest pit of her pupils.

"I never thought you wouldn't come through with the money, Seb, it wasn't about that, the contract. It was about…it was about…it was about not giving you the chance to break my heart."

"I'm not going to do that, sweetheart. I promise you." I grip her soft hand in mine, squeezing it with every word, hoping she'll believe me.

She looks down at the cash receipt, and up at me. "Can we really do this?"

I tuck my finger under her chin, lifting her pure, sweet face to look at me. "Is it what you want?"

She nods and my heart does a backflip.

"Then yes, we can, just trust me." And I lean in and kiss her softly.

I pull away and she shakes her head sadly. "I don't know how."

I smile and graze her cheek with the side of my finger.

"I'm going to show you."

And before she can change her mind, I grab her hand and pull her to her feet.

"Come on!" I pull her out of the classroom. "Come on!"

"Where are we going?" she pants, trying to keep up with me.

"Does it matter?" I ask.

And her sweet laugh tells me it doesn't.

***

"Are we there yet?" she asks for the tenth time, twisting around in her car seat, trying to figure out our destination.

"Where is 'there'?"

"I don't know!" she yells and faux glares at me.

"I know, so stop trying to get me to tell you!" I laugh.

She pouts and I lean over to kiss her and she melts against me. In the space of an hour, somehow kissing her has become like the most natural thing I've ever done. More natural than sleep, more natural than playing the cello. I was born to kiss her.

"Green light, asshole!" She pushes me away, laughing. And I'm glad that there's no testing for being drunk on sound.

"Oops, SORRY," I wave to the car behind me honking its horn.

They say you never really know what you've got 'til it's gone, or that you don't really know the best part of your life while you're living it, but someone must've imbibed me with some sort of hindsight superpower, because I know, this last hour, sitting in this car and being in her presence, is easily the best hour of my life so far.

After she'd finally stopped fighting me and let me lead her to my car, we'd stopped for a moment, looking at each other, wondering if we were really going to do this. She'd reached up and touched my face, and I'd turned my cheek to press a kiss to her palm. Taking her palm and then pressing my kiss to her heart, and I knew what she was thinking, whatever happens, it'd be worth it for that moment.

"Sebbbbbbbbbbbbbb, where are we going?" she moans and I can't help but chuckle at her childlike curiosity.

"You'll see...in... about.... fifteen seconds," I tell her.

We pass a sign and I see her head whip around, trying to read it.

"Bankkkkstownn... Airport...Wait. Airport? Where are WE GOING?!?!?!" Her excitement level gets turbocharged and she jumps up and down in her seat.

"Huh? Who said anything about the airport?" I say, trying to hide the excitement in my own voice.

"Oh." She instantly deflates, and I have to turn my head away from her so she doesn't see my grin. She goes quiet as she tries to hide her disappointment.

That is, until she sees me turn into the Bankstown Airport driveway.

"OMYGOD, we ARE going somewhere! WHERE?!"

I ignore her and drive down until we're just outside the main entrance.

She jumps out of the car before I can get out and open the door for her. Her eyes are bright as she searches my face for answers. I wrap her up in my arms, pulling her jiggling body up against me, enjoying her softness, her warmth.

She stops her jumping for a moment and lifts her face to mine, kissing me softly, letting out a soft sigh. Then she whispers, "Where are we going?" Her relentless curiosity is so sweet and I can't help answering. "Anywhere you want."

She pulls away, confused, "What? How?"

"We can go anywhere in the world you want." I reach into my back pocket and pull out our passports. She takes them from me, staring at me open-mouthed. I press a kiss to her forehead and continue, "All you have to do is tell that pilot. He's been waiting. Now I'm going to have to pay him extra because you took so long arguing with me in your classroom."

She opens her mouth even wider. And closes it. I can see her mind working, and I press another soft kiss to her temple.

"I know where I want to go!" And she pulls out of my embrace and runs off to the pilot.

"Wait, where?" I call after her.

"Ha! Now it's your turn not to know." She pokes her tongue out at me and skips off to whisper in the ear of the pilot I'd pointed to.

"Witch!" I shout to her, running up to catch up with her, my body feeling lighter than it ever has.

Chapter Seventeen

SEBASTIAN

"Sebbie?" she calls me by the nickname I've hated my whole life until just then.

"Yes, Mary?" I retaliate.

She scrunches her face up for a moment, then continues. "Push me out of the plane."

"No," I answer, "Anything else?"

"But I want to die," she says surprisingly, but if I know anything about her by now, there's a reason for it, that will come in its own good time.

"Maybe later."

"Ok, but promise me you'll think about it," she pleads.

"How 'bout this? If you keep eating those chocolates and don't leave me any, I'll not only think about it, I'll do it, film it and put it on YouTube."

"YAY!" She raises her hands in celebration of her strange victory.

"Why do you want to die?" I have to ask.

"I'm just so, so happy. Everything's gotta be downhill from here," she explains, sighing.

My heart warms and I reach across the little table between us to squeeze her hand. "Oh. In that case, let's just jump out of the plane together."

"THEN who will film us?"

"We'll post on Facebook that we're doing it...naked... then there'll be no shortage of people filming it."

"Pfft, filming you maybe," she scoffs.

"What do you mean?"

"Who'd want to see ME naked?" she snickers.

I look at her like she's crazy. Because she must be. Right now, with her legs tucked up under her, her sweet, curvy ass in the air as she's bent over staring out the window in our private plane, I've literally had to tighten my seatbelt about three times just to stop me from getting up and ravaging her in that very position.

"Hey!" I say loudly and she jumps a little, startled. "Get that sexy ass over here."

She grins and blushes a little. I nod and she climbs off her seat and looks around.

"Don't worry, no one's coming."

"Oh yeah, they're used to your flight booty calls, no doubt," she jokes, and then her face darkens a little, and my chest twinges a little to see it.

I undo my seatbelt and reach for her hand, pulling her towards me and she stumbles and falls into my lap.

"Hey..." I say, softer this time. "Look at me."

Her face angles down so our eyes lock, her hair tumbles down around us, creating a curtain and enveloping us in our own private little world.

"You are so goddamned beautiful that I hired some strange man who claims to be a pilot and told him to take me anywhere in the world you told him to go and didn't even try to get it out of you. That's how insanely fucking gorgeous you are. And I haven't even seen you naked yet. But I'm hoping my first time won't be as we're hurtling to our deaths, but if it comes to that, so be it. I ain't dying without see that."

"Oh, Sebbie," she says and clutches at her heart. "It's a good thing you do instrumental covers of love songs...because that's the most unromantic thing I've ever heard!" And she falls off my lap and to the floor laughing.

"Erm." I nudge her with my foot. "Excuse me."

She only laughs louder as my toe pokes her in the side and apparently catches the attention of our flight attendant.

"Um, can I help you with something?" she peeks through the curtain and looks down at the cackling woman on the floor of the cabin,

"Um, just some more tonic, thank you." I say calmly and smile at her as she glances once more at Cadence before leaving to get my drink.

"Hey! Crazy!" I get up and stand over her, one foot on each side of her hips.

She stops laughing for a moment and lies back on her back and looks up at me. Her eyes look lit up like Christmas lights and her cheeks are flushed from her laughing fit. Her neck glistens a little from a light sweat and I just want to bury my face in the carpet of soft curls framing her face.

She reached a hand towards me and I take it, letting her pull me down onto the floor with her. I lay down and she curls up against me, her leg draping over mine and her head on my chest.

"Can we stay up here forever?" she whispers against my neck, and her breath makes the hair stand up on my spine, so sweet, so sexy.

"We might have to; I don't know where we're going." I run my fingers through her hair and she rests her chin on my chest, looking up at me.

"You'll see."

"I can wait, I'm in no hurry to be anywhere but right here with you."

She sighs a long deep sigh. "That's much better. See? You CAN be romantic."

"I sure can. Now show me your boobs!" I say and reach over and squeeze her gently on the chest.

"Um," a third voice suddenly speaks up, "I'll just put your drink here, sir."

And it's ten minutes before Cadence finally stops laughing again.

CADENCE

If I were to be abducted by aliens, probed and then brainwashed by their technology and finally returned to earth after a hundred years, I would still remember the look on Sebastian's face when he looked out the window as we flew over Uluru.

"Oh my god," he'd sighed, and I'd had to agree with the sentiment.

"It's nothing like I imagined it would be," he'd finally uttered after staring out the window in awe for the minutes the pilot circled the great red rock.

I'd only nodded. The experience of Uluru is a personal and unique one, and I didn't want to influence his in any way.

"Thank you." He turned to me as the pilot finally flew towards the Ayers Rock airport.

I hadn't said anything, because if anyone owed anyone a thank you, it would be me to him.

We'd just stared out our respective windows and watched the red sky sink into the red earth.

***

"The car will be ready in a minute," Sebastian comes back after talking to the car hire guy at the booth.

"Ok, and the hotel room's ready any time we get there. It's about fifteen minutes from here."

He nods and pulls me in against him, his hand resting against the small of my back. Since leaving Sydney, it seems he can't stop touching me, wanting to be close to me. And there's no reason for me to complain. I've left all my worries and concerns back in the classroom.

"You tired?" He says gently, caressing my cheek.

"No, I'm good. Happy." I give him a smile to reassure him.

"Regret your choice?"

"No, I love it here."

"I didn't mean about the location. I meant…about the choice of company."

I open my mouth to make a joke and then stop, realizing he doesn't have any reason to trust me more than me him, and it's not the time to test that.

"No. Except, maybe, that I didn't make it sooner."

***

It's dark when we load ourselves into the rental car. The hire guy tells us that our resort isn't far from there but to make sure we have our cell phone charged because there's hardly any traffic at this time of day and into the night, and if we need help, the best thing is to call rather than wait for help.

"You ready?" Sebastian asks once I've clicked in my seatbelt.

"As I'll ever be!"

We drive in a comfortable silence for a moment. It's almost pitch black once we leave the main highway, and I look out into the dark and wonder what is looking back at me. It's unnerving but somehow poetic at the same time. The refocus of our senses when any stimulation of one sense is completely nil. It reminds me a little of the opening of the band's intro.

Our ruminations are interrupted by the vibration of his phone.

"Seb, we said no phones," I remind him, when he takes his eyes off the road for a moment to glance at his phone.

"I just...I just have to take this one call, sorry," he says before swerving to the side of the road and pressing the answer button on the phone.

"Hey," he says.

And I can hear the female voice reply. It's Hailey.

"Hey, what's up?" Her tinny voice through the earpiece says.

"Yeah, um, just letting you guys know that Cadence and I won't be at rehearsal until Monday, probably. Can you let your Dad and the guys know? And I won't be reachable until then either."

There's a pause.

"Why?" she asks, and I turn towards my window, hiding the scrunched up look on my face.

"Just tell them, Hails."

"You okay?"

"Better than ever." I hear him reply and he pokes me gently in the back.

"You with her?"

"okay, relay the message, okay? Thanks. Talk to you soon."

He hangs up the phone and turns to me. "All done, no more calls, I promise."

I can't face him yet, so I continue staring out into the dark.

"Hey, you okay?"

"She's always going to come between us, isn't she?"

"What are you talking about?"

"Hailey."

"Oh god, not this again."

"Yes, exactly, that's exactly what I think. Every time."

"I told you. There's nothing –" he starts to deny.

I cut him off, "No, listen to me. You might not have any feelings for her, I don't know, but she definitely does for you, and she makes no effort to hide it."

"You're crazy," he scoffs and runs his hands through this hair.

"Do you know she's supposedly slept with half the band?"

"No. She hasn't."

"Yes, she has. She said it herself! Sarah heard her bragging about it in the bathroom."

"Look, I get that women are weird around her, but I told you, there's never been anything between us. What you're seeing is just very close friends. She's been on tour with us, in the hard times and the good times, that's all it is."

"Well, I can't compete with that..." I admit, and suddenly, I'm so tired.

"You don't have to."

"I just...I need some air..."

I throw open the door and step outside. It's suddenly cold and I wrap my arms around me.

"Cadence! Get back in the car!"

I ignore him and hear his car door open and his footsteps crunching in the dirt as he runs over to me.

"Cadence!" He grabs me from behind and pulls me hard against him, his face burying in the back of my neck.

I try not to melt against him, reaching up to brush a tear from my eyes. "Why is this so hard, Sebastian?"

"It doesn't have to be. Just trust me, why can't you just trust me?" He spins me around and in the dark, I can just make out his face through my tear-filled eyes.

"Make me. Give me no other choice, Sebastian. Make me not care, make it so nothing else matters, the fear, the distrust, the not knowing. Make it so...I can't help but be with you."

His eyes burn into me, and I'm suddenly hot.

"Goddammit, Cadence, don't you know how much I want you? How hard it's been this last month to force myself to hold back from you? Do you? Do you know how much it physically hurt not to just bury myself inside you? How much I wanted to make you mine and only mine for all time?

"I don't believe you," I say and he growls.

I run my fingertips over my lips then reach out and press them against his mouth.

"Show me."

Those two words release him from any restraint he ever enforced on himself.

He grabs my arms around the biceps and pushes me back against the car. Tucking his hand under my ass he lifts me up and wraps my legs around his waist. Leaning me back against the car door, he drags his lips along the line of my neck.

I feel his teeth graze the skin. A moan comes from somewhere, and I think it's me. My hands come up to tangle in his hair and I feel his hand run along my thighs as he tightens them around his waist.

"Cadence. Baby, you drive me so crazy," he groans as I grind against him.

His tongue is hot against the valley between my breasts as he drags his head up to meet mine, pausing for just a moment to take a breath before ravaging my mouth with his.

Lost in his kiss, I barely feel him reach between us to fumble with his zipper.

"God, I'm so fucking hard. You have no idea how much I've dreamt of this, Cadence."

I can't even tell him, that I've fantasized about him just as much. His mouth is suddenly everywhere, on my mouth, on my neck, suckling my nipples through the thin material of my dress. My back arches, cleaving to him, wanting more, wanting every inch of my body, my skin to feel his.

"Make me yours, Sebastian," I hear myself rasp.

He growls and I feel his hands fumble with my skirt, pushing it up my thighs to bunch at my waist. And suddenly, his fingers are inside me. I feel myself part, taking him in, feeling him make his way deeper and deeper.

"Fuck," he groans, and I can't breathe for wanting him.

"Are you this wet for me?" He wants to know. I can only groan in response.

"Are you ready for me?" he asks, pressing the ball of his hand against me, driving his finger in deeper. I hold back a moan and nod and bite my lip. I've been ready for him for weeks. I feel him reach into his pocket and the sound of a foil wrapper tearing.

And then suddenly he stops. Leaning over me, he stares me in the eyes, they're darker than I've ever seen them, and I just want to dive inside them.

He kisses me softly, a moment of sweetness that makes my heart dance, and gently touches the side of my face.

Then just as I'm about to whisper his name, I feel him position his hips, and slide all the way inside me.

The breath catches in my throat, and I almost choke. His cock is thick and hard, and he's driving himself as far as he can into the core of me. My body tenses and contracts, trying to make room for him, but it's not meant to be easy. Fucking him is exactly what I thought it would be, hard, furious, overwhelming.

All I know is that with every thrust he's filing me up, more and more, and I'm taking him, deeper and deeper, making him mine as well as becoming his.

"Cadence, baby, Cadence. You are so sexy. Take me, please, just take me," he moans over and over.

I arch my back and meet his thrust with a grind of my hips and he roars, and the sound echoes in the dark. I lift myself up by pulling on his neck, rocking my hips and he growls his approval. Each motion has him grazing against my aching bud and I know it's coming.

I can feel it, in the pit of my stomach, feel it build.

He pace quickens and I know he's right there with me.

My legs tighten around his waist and his thrusts become shorter and faster, each one pushing me closer and closer.

His breath cools the sweat dripping on my neck.

"Oh, god, Sebastian,"

"Yes, yes, yes…"

And then, something breaks inside me, and a flood of pleasure spreads like wildfire from the roots of my scalp through every cell in my body.

I hear a faraway scream and Sebastian pulling my body into his arms. He grunts again and again and his hips grinds against mine, and I feel him explode, his body shaking and shattering.

He crushes my mouth with his and our breaths and lips fight to find room around our climax.

I fall limp back against the car and he leans against me, my legs still loosely gripped around his waist.

I try to catch my breath, but it's only coming in short spurts. My body is still convulsing from the receding waves of orgasm.

My eyes closed, I feel his head rest on my chest, his breathing short and fast.

I wonder if it happened after all, that he pushed me out of that plane, and that was me falling and falling into him and this eternity of pleasure.

Sebastian's hands come up to hold up my legs, my muscle power all but lost.

"So, I guess we can really consider our contract null and void."

I giggle and run my fingers through his hair, pulling his head back down to me for a kiss.

"Hmmmm."

"Maybe we can write up a new one instead," I suggest.

"Ok. That one will be easy."

"Yeah? What do you think I should put in it?"

"Just the one line: Cadence's wish is Seb's command."

I sigh and tremble from the aftermath. "In that case…I would like to invoke the terms of our contract."

"Ohh? You little minx." He tickles my neck with his tongue and I feel his finger slip through the drenched folds of my sex. "And what is that?"

"Feed me! I'm so bloody hungry!"

He roars with laughter and I can't help but think how it sounds even better than his cello playing.

Chapter Eighteen

SEBASTIAN

It's been about thirty minutes since I was inside her, and it seems like thirty minutes is now the definition of an eternity. A forever just waiting to feel her wrapped around me, giving and taking all at once. On the other hand, I don't think I'll ever forget the feel of her lips against mine, crushing them, imprinting the shape of her mouth on mine, the sounds of her need, her urgency, the metallic taste of blood as her teeth grazed my tongue, biting me.

Returning to the car, our breaths fogging up the windows, I turn to her, and she looks just the same. Beautiful in her flushed, just fucked glory. But still the Cadence I'd been lost in all these weeks.

But what had changed is me.

I don't know what will happen if my life returns to a state when I can't just lean over and kiss her whenever my heart desires.

***

"Is this okay?"

She turns to me, her face slightly worried but excited at once.

We've parked outside a luxurious little bungalow, the last in a series of similar units, the roof shaped like a beige sand sail, and the balcony opening up into the open space of the Northern Territory. It looks spacious and intimate all at once.

I'd given her my credit card at the airport and told her to go all out. I didn't know what to expect, but I don't know why I'd be surprised she'd pick anything less than perfect. Her regarding my taste was spot on.

"Come here," I hold my hand out to her and she skips over to me, and I hold her face in my hands. "This is perfect," I reassure her. "I love it. I really do. But even if it was just a corrugated roof over a cardboard box, if you were there, it would be just as perfect."

She sighs happily and I kiss her sweet upturned mouth.

"But THIS one has champagne!" and she runs into the bungalow, ooohing and ahhhing at all the amenities.

I laugh and carry our bags into the room and lay down on the bed, stretching out, feeling my muscles groan and my bones crack. I haven't slept in days, laying awake the last week trying to figure out what to do about Cadence. This morning when I called the accountant and told him to organize the bank check, I could not have possibly imagined that it would turn out this way. Me in her arms and her ingrained in my heart.

"Sebastian! There's a waterfall shower! I love those!" she twitters happily from the adjoining bathroom.

I smile, my face sore for doing so for the last few hours we've been together. But her infectious love of life is unavoidable and she's warmed me from inside out like the morning sun on a scorching hot summer day.

"Ooooh! Toothpaste!" she squeals and I can't help but chuckle.

"What?" she asks, her voice muffled probably from rubbing her face against something.

"Nothing, darling, you brush your teeth as much as you like, if we run out, I'll call the front desk for some more." I tease her, but I think she's too excited to care.

"Ohh," she sighs as she comes back into the bedroom and sinks onto the bed at my feet. She reaches for my shoes and pulls them off, peeling the socks off after that. "Thank god you're rich! Or else we'd have had to go to buy our own toothpaste."

I laugh, sometimes I forget that I am, which is strange because I certainly wasn't always well off. But sometimes, I'm glad I am, just for moment like this, to bring a smile to the faces of people I care about.

She kicks off her own shoes and falls down onto the bed, curling up around me and resting her head on my chest. She reaches over my body for my hand and interweaves her fingers with mine.

It is quiet.

Not a whisper of a breath of wind quiet.

No wild animals foraging or calling for their mates quiet.

No white hum from the moonlight quiet.

It's some time before I realize I've been holding my breath too.

"Babe?" I nudge her gently.

"Mmm?" She mumbles sleepily and curls up in a tighter ball around me, her hand growing limp and sliding from mine to tuck under her head.

I tilt my head to press a kiss to her forehead and whisper a gentle "good night". The quiet engulfs me and soon I am breathing deeply too, and dreaming of round brown eyes and floating on clouds.

***

Something delicious is happening. That's the absolute first thought I have when I wake up.

Something that is making my eyes water and my mouth dry at the same time.

Something that is weighing on my breath and causing my fingers to clench.

Something that is warm and wet, making the pit of my stomach start to burn, to churn.

Something that feels sweet like just whipped chocolate mousse but hot like chili oil searing the top of your mouth.

Something that makes me moan without me knowing I'm doing it.

And then, for a moment it stops.

"It's about time you woke up," I hear Cadence taunt me, and then I feel the deliciousness again.

Her mouth is sliding down my cock, my already achingly hard, engorged to a straining thickness cock.

Oh my god, I process, as my head falls back onto the pillow, my fucking cock is in Cadence's fucking mouth.

And fuck me if she doesn't know what she's doing.

Undoing me, that's what she's doing.

My fingers curl and grip the bed sheet as the tip of my cock grazes the back of her throat.

Oh. My. God.

She drags her lips up the length of my hardness and I struggle to take a breath. She giggles and runs her fingertip around the rim of my dick.

"Stop." I don't know why I say it. Which is good because she doesn't listen.

Instead, I feel her hand wrap itself at the base of my shaft and then her lips, those soft, moist, plump, fucking lips from heaven, drop around the head of my cock and then slide back down, completely engulfing me in her mouth.

I arch my back and try to thrust deeper.

She gags gently, and the sound sends me into a downward spiral.

I tilt my head to watch her. She's kneeling between my legs, her ass bobbing in the air as she attends to my iron hard cock. I need to come.

"Climb on me, baby," I rasp, reaching for her.

She pulls off my cock and I almost regret interrupting her. But there's plenty of time for that. Right now, I want to be inside her again.

Straddling over me, she pulls her t-shirt off, and her tits fall, fleshy and pump on my face as she leans over, angling her nipples to rest on my lips. I suckle at them hungrily. They instantly harden and I flick the tips with my tongue. Her groan is my reward and I do it again so I can burn that delicious sound into my brain.

I feel her lean and brace her hands on either side of my face and her hips move into position. I reach around her and run the tip of my cock along the opening of her sex. It's burning hot. The little minx woke me up so I could do this for her.

Lifting my hips, she moans softly at the pressure of my cock and she pushes herself off her hands and rocks back onto her heels, sinking all the way down on my shaft.

I'm going to last about five more seconds.

If I'm lucky.

No man was ever meant to hold back from this kind of pleasure.

"Fuck me, baby," I growl and I grab her ass in my hands, lifting her off my cock. She rocks back and forth and I think my cock is about to explode. Her tits bounce and I'm mesmerized watching them.

"Sebastian...fuck, Sebastian." Did my name always sound like that? I don't have time to think about it.

"Fuck, Fuck, FUCK!" I yell just as I feel the pressure in my balls release and I'm thrusting up into her, deeper and deeper. Maybe if I go so deep, I never have to leave. My orgasm bursts through my body and I stop breathing as I feel myself empty inside her. Inside her delicious, sweet, velvet cave.

I let go of her ass and reach between us to pinch her sweet little bud with my fingers. It's all she needs.

Throwing her head back, she screams my name and I watch her body shake and shake and shake as she climaxes. Until she collapses on top of me, her face like an iron against my skin, her breath hot and heavy.

The soft orange hue of sunrise is filtering through the windows and she looks just like an angel.

"Good morning," I whisper.

"Morning," she mumbles, her face still buried in my chest.

She takes a deep breath and shuffles up a little higher on my body, and we sigh, feeling me slip out of her.

She smiles and kisses me, making a little "hmmm" noise that I'm becoming addicted to.

"So, what do you want to do today?" I ask her.

"That." She grins.

I laugh. Not that I mind. "We just did 'that.'"

"So? Let's do it again." She grins even wider and reaches down to fondle me.

"Exactly 'that' might take a few minutes, but there are other versions of 'that' that I might be able to interest you in?"

"Oh? I'm open to suggestions."

I flip her over and slide down her body, kissing her as I go.

Gently pressing her legs wide apart, I lay between them, lowering my mouth to her soft, glistening lips, "Oh, open is just how I want you to be," and I graze my tongue along her slit.

I can't quite make out her response, but I think she likes it.

Chapter Nineteen

CADENCE

If you cut me open, you'll see me bleed red earth.

Not gush out in thick rivulets, but in dust whirls, small tornados carrying my body and spirit into the wind, scattering me over this beautiful, burnt, vast, dry, copper red land.

I may be first generation Australian, a child of immigrants, but the day I was born, the first breath of air I inhaled carried with it tens of thousands of years of Australian history and tied me forever in with the people and the land, so that my story would start and end here.

And it's why I brought Sebastian here, of all the places in the world, it's here I wanted us to come, to be the place where we would get to know each other.

Amongst the harsh heat of the desert sun, and the crisp cold breeze of night.

With the echoes of the spirits of the Aboriginal people around to witness the promises our bodies and hearts made to each other, and bind us together with their blessings.

***

"Cadence! LOOK!" Sebastian parks the Jeep on the side of an abandoned paddock and quickly jumps out, pointing his phone camera out into the horizon.

"What?" I call after him.

"It's a kangaroo!! With a little joey!" he squeals, and I can't help but laugh at his childlike excitement.

"Er, yeah, we have a few of those around," I tease him, secretly committing the squeal to memory.

I lean on the hood of the car, watching him run a few steps and then stop, trying to get close to the mama kangaroo and her baby. After posing for a few photos, she gets sick of him and bounces off lazily, in no rush to get away from the human.

He jogs back to me, his face split open into a giant grin, waving his camera. "Got her! Oh, that was so cool."

"Yeah, I guess you don't see too many roos jumping down the Champs-Élysée."

"Pfft, even if they did, Parisians would just scoff and say they'd seen it all before."

"Maybe on their dinner plates!"

"Quoi? You don't EAT kangaroos here, do you?" He looks like I've just suggested we eat a human baby.

I shrug, "Sure, not a lot but yeah, you can get kangaroo meat at any grocery store."

He turns to me, absolutely horrified. "You are savages! Cute little kangaroos hopping around, you catch them and then EAT them?"

"What are you so horrified about; you eat foie gras!"

"That's goose, geese aren't cute! They don't carry their adorable baby geese in a front bag."

"Front bag?" I'm confused. Sometimes I forget that English isn't his first language until he comes up with something golden like this.

"You know, the hole in their furry tummy."

"You mean 'pouch'?" I spit out.

"Whatever, savage."

"Which reminds me, you owe me breakfast...and dinner! You didn't feed me last night after all that show and dance about Cadence's wish is your command."

"You fell asleep, honey." He shrugs and doesn't look at all apologetic.

"But then I woke up."

"Did you ever!" He grins and winks at me, and my legs instantly feel a little wobbly.

"Come on, I know of a great place you can make it up to me," I tell him, to distract me from thoughts that would have me forgetting about breakfast and dinner altogether.

"Oh no, I'm going to need some sustenance," he groans.

"Not that, you perv! Food!" I squawk at him and he laughs until a camera bag thwacks him on the head.

***

"It's definitely alien," Sebastian says after a few minutes of rare quiet.

"It's not alien."

"Then where did it come from?"

"The sky."

"Yeah, an alien dropped it," he insists.

"An alien. Picked up Uluru...and then accidentally dropped it," I have to repeat it just to make sure I've heard him correctly.

"Sure, a giant alien. With slippery hands."

I have to put my glass down, to keep from spilling it as I hold my stomach with my other hand as I bend over in laughter.

"What? Do YOU have a better explanation?" he asks, looking hurt.

"There are thousands of years of better explanations than that."

"Well, I guess we'll never know."

"I think we know it's not a giant alien with crappy finger grip that created Uluru."

"It's not my fault you have so little faith." He sniffs, and turns back to observing the stunning horizon.

"I'm here, aren't I?"

We're sitting on our balcony looking out as the sun sets over the giant red rock, that under the angle of light looks like it's sprouted a halo, illuminating it against the darkening sky.

We can hear the sound of our neighbors enjoying their own meal and experiencing the unique experience of the sun setting over Uluru.

I shove an olive-oil-soaked piece of bread into my mouth; part of the array of food we'd picked up at the store, our makeshift gourmet dinner picnic.

"Hmmm, so good," I say and dip another piece and hold it out to Sebastian.

He opens his mouth and as I push the bread into his mouth, he clamps his lips down, trapping my fingers and then slowly licks the oil dripping off them.

"Hmm, you're right, delicious," he winks at me. My nipples harden instantly and I wonder if there'll ever be a time my body's not going to react to him from the smallest things.

He watches me eat for a moment, and I let him, somehow feeling so comfortable in his presence that I don't really care that he sees me spitting out olive pits and sucking on lamb chop bones.

"When's the first time you came here?" he asks, picking up his fork and stabbing a cherry tomato dancing around his plate.

"It's a long story."

"I don't have anywhere to be and you've sexed me out for a while, so, spill," he presses, already used to my evasive tactics.

I take a sip of wine and sit back, looking out at the scenery. "When I was ten, my grandmother died after a pretty long illness. After the funeral, we were in the car, and suddenly, my Dad spins the car around and he says, 'where do you want to go? Anywhere in the world.'"

I take a bite of some bread and chew it for a few seconds.

"Just like me?" Sebastian asks.

"Just like you, except that, I don't think he quite meant it. We didn't have luggage or passports or anything. Anyway, as we're driving into the airport there are those signs advertising places, and I saw a picture of Uluru. So, we walk up to the sales desk and they ask, how can I help you, and I say 'Uluru!' And five hours later, here we were. Well, not here here, we weren't millionaires... but yes, here near Uluru."

"That's amazing."

"Yeah, it was an amazing trip." I nod and smile, even now remembering stepping off the plane and feeling so glamorous and world travelled. Having that power to just pick a place in the world, it made me feel a like a princess. And Sebastian had recreated that for me. A moment he didn't even know was one of the best of my life.

"Sounds like it."

"He was an amazing dad."

"Was?"

I take another sip of wine, savoring it in my mouth for a moment before I speak again. "Yeah, he, er, he died when I was fourteen years old."

"Oh, Cadence," Sebastian sighs, sensing the loss it was for me at such a young age.

"He was the one who taught me to play piano. It took me a long, long time to find another teacher after he died."

"He'd be so fucking proud if he could see you now."

"What about yours?" I turn the questioning back to me.

"He'd be proud of you too if he knew you." Sebastian winks and grins, and I almost let him get away with it, the way his mouth curls into that irresistible cheekiness. But I don't.

"Hey, I shared…"

"I don't have any romantic lovey stories to tell you about my dad. He's a rough, tough guy."

"He's not proud of what you've achieved with the band?"

He pops a chip into his mouth and crunches for a moment, thinking the question over. "I guess not. You know, I think it might have to do with his pride. Growing up, we didn't have fuck all, sometimes not even a roof over our heads, and he could not stand me not just leaving school and going off making money as a laborer or something. When I got the scholarship to Guildhall Music in London, he couldn't use the tuition as an excuse to make me leave, and we pretty much stopped talking for years."

The thought of having such a relationship with your father is so foreign to me, and I wonder how that must affect him now.

"Do you talk now?"

"Not really, some, I guess. I go home to visit my mom. And he always brings out these fucking scrapbooks with clipping of the band and making comments about how we dress and the songs we pick for our performance, and how we could always do better. Like he knows. Nitpicking over interviews and everything!"

I smile at him, listening to him rant. "You don't get it, do you?"

"What?"

I lean over the table between us and he meets me halfway, pressing a gentle kiss to my lips.

"Sometimes you have to read between the lines."

A blank look spreads across Sebastian's face and I can't help but feel a thrill as I get to embed a whole new series of expressions of his into my Sebastian Face Bank.

"You say he has scrapbooks of clippings of your shows and interviews..." I say, nudging him towards his own revelation.

"Yeah, tens of them, we're in the paper? You name it, he's found it and cut it out. To point out everything that's fucking wrong I've done."

"Sebastian, sometimes people express love...and pride in different ways. But I don't see a father who couldn't give a fuck about his kid cutting out hundreds of clippings, do you?"

He goes quiet and I pour us each another glass of wine.

The expression on his face changes again, and I wish I could peer inside his mind and hear his thought. The sky mimics his face and changes from burnt orange and almost neon pink to the various shades of dark before slipping into night.

Eventually, he gets up and holds out his hand to me.

"Come with me."

I slide my fingers against his palm without hesitation. "Where are we going?"

He tugs on my hand and pulls me to me feet, spinning me around, burying his face against my neck. I shiver as he breathes, and the air wafts against the sweat on my skin.

"Into the bedroom. I need to be inside you," he growls, dragging his tongue against the curve of my neck, pulling gently on the sleeve of my shirt to expose more skin.

My nipples harden instantly and he slides a finger down to play with the straining tip.

"Why?" I rasp, wanting to hear him voice his desire for me.

"Because you're so brilliant, I need to be a part of you."

Despite the heat of his words, I can't help but feel my heart warm because of the sentiment. His finger on my nipples distracts me from any thoughts not related to what he's doing, however, and my head falls back, my chest arching, my body using its movements to beg for more.

He spins me around again, so I'm facing him, and he drops to his knees in front of me. Pulling my skirt up to my hips, he buries his face against the cotton of my panties, the heat from his breath already drawing the moisture from my sex.

I run my fingers through his hair and rock my hips against his face.

"And what about me? Where am I going?" I ask him, knowing I'm already on my way.

"To heaven and back, baby," he promises, as his fingers push my underwear to the side and he slips his tongue against the pulsing, aching bud between my legs.

And I did.

Again and again and again.

Chapter Twenty

SEBASTIAN

"It's time," I say to her, as we lay there, clothes and bed sheets twisted between our legs and sweaty, sex-ravaged bodies. Her head is on my chest and my fingers in her hair, my heart on my sleeve and hers in my trust.

"For what?" she mumbles, her lips moving against the dip in my sternum.

"For you to tell me what happened."

"What happened when?"

"What happened that you, even you, have trouble trusting. You, who have faith in music and air and smiles and friendship. But not me, not men."

She sighs and I run a finger down the length of her arm. Wanting the contact to give her strength. Strength to tell me, to trust me, to relive it.

"I came…really, really close to not wanting to live any more. Seriously close," she says.

I freeze. I can't imagine those words coming from her. From my Cadence.

"What did you say?" I eventually have to ask her to repeat herself, to clarify.

"I said," she repeats, in a steady voice, "I almost killed myself."

"When? Why?" I sit up, and she follows, pulling the sheet up around her and pushing the hair from her face.

"Why do people tend to commit suicide? They just don't want to live any more. And there was a time…I just didn't."

"My god, what happened?"

"Long or short story?" She asks, as if there's really a choice.

"I don't think the short story exists."

"No, and I guess it deserves a long story." She shuffles around on the bed, leaning back on the headboard and I wait. I have no right to rush this.

"I'll start by stating this. I'm fine now. I've been fine for a long time. But for a while there, I wasn't. I was the furthest thing from fine. So, we were living in Melbourne at the time and I had just turned fourteen and my Dad had just passed away. My mum and I had moved to a different school because we couldn't afford the house we were living in anymore. On the first day of school, in music class, of course, music class, I got paired up with this guy, his name was Brent. He was a drummer."

"Why am I not surprised?" I give her a soft squeeze on the arm, and she smiles softly.

"You shouldn't be. No one was. Let's just say, I was a little less...well, pink cardigan-y, back then. Anyway, we dated for three years, all through high school, and we applied to the Sydney Music Conservatory together. We were destined, or so we thought. Turns out music talent wasn't all they were looking for, some dedication to actual schoolwork was needed, something Brent didn't have. Anyway, cliché of all clichés, I got in and he didn't. "

"Ah, his ego must've liked that." I cocked my head. I can only imagine how her boyfriend would've taken that, being of an ego-driven nature myself.

"Nothing about him liked that. But there wasn't going to be anything that stopped me from going. As much as I loved him...I had my dad's memory to keep alive."

She takes a breath, to remember her father, I feel, and I can't take my eyes off her. What had happened to this amazing woman? And yet here she still was, with a heart the size of that giant sunburnt rock out there.

She shifts and I know she's ready to continue.

"So, the closer the day came to me going to Sydney, the colder and more distant he became. He started drinking, something he'd never done before and I'm sure that drugs started coming into the picture as well. I just thought it was...I don't know, I thought that once he realized it wasn't going to be so bad, he still had his music, he was in an up-and-coming band, Uni wasn't ever really his thing anyway, and we could visit every month, he'd calm down. Every day he still kept begging me to stay, saying he couldn't live without me, and me, in my youth, thought that it was almost sweet, romantic even."

"But he didn't calm down?" God, what did this fuckhead do to her? I already want to bash him for trying to hold her back.

"No. No, he did not. Two days before I was supposed to go, my mother threw me a going away party, all my friends and family, pretty much everyone I'd ever met in my life. In hindsight, he was weird that night, more than he had been in the week leading up to it. Like, he was strangely calm and sweet even. I thought he'd finally come around. Then just as my mom brought out the cake, he asked to say a few words. I was so touched, he wasn't really a man of words..."

She stops and I can see her eyes glaze over for a moment, as if she's physically trying to brace herself for what's to come. I want to reach out to touch her, but something stops me, like, she wants to get this over and done with, and to put it in the past.

"We'd had pictures projecting on the walls all night, and then, just as he goes up, the pictures stop. And the images change. But I hear it even before it focuses. I can hear the sounds. I can hear myself moaning and breathing. It's dark and blurry, but there's no mistaking it. It's a video of him and me having sex. On the wall, for everyone to see."

"Oh, Cadence." Oh god.

"And everyone is just frozen. I was looking at him, and he had the biggest smirk on his face. And then someone, I don't know who, covers the projector, but you can still hear the sounds. And then he just says into the microphone, 'It's okay. For those who want to know how it ends, it's now on every popular porn site. And your email.' Then he drops the mic and comes up to me and says, 'no one leaves me. I leave them. And I'm leaving you. I can't be tangled up with a two-bit porn slut.'"

She stops, her eyes are blurry from the tears falling and I have to grip my fingers into fists to stop from brushing them away. I know there's more, and she had to get through it without me interfering.

"I didn't even find out until a few days later that he'd somehow managed to send the link to the video to everyone at the University in Sydney as well. It didn't take me more than one morning to know that I couldn't be there. Not just because of the humiliation, but it wasn't even safe. I was harassed everywhere I went. About two days in, a guidance counselor told me that they thought it'd be better if I took a semester off. To let things settle down."

She reaches over to the side table for a tissue and locks her eyes with mine for a moment, then looks away.

"I went back to Melbourne with my tail between my legs. For three months, I didn't leave the house. I didn't talk to anyone except my mother. But...they still came. I don't know where they came from, but they were everywhere?"

"Who?"

"All sorts. People who want to hire me for their porn sites, people who wanted to hurt me. People who just liked seeing my embarrassment, and people who got off on my pain. Strangers. Some acquaintances, I guess, but mostly strangers. Sick assholess who had nothing better to do in their lives than elongate my humiliation."

I look down at her hands and they've shredded the damp tissue. And I feel like doing the same to the heads of the people who'd hurt her.

"I went deep and dark. I felt like I'd lost everything I'd worked for, and there was no going back. I could not see a light at the end of the tunnel, it just kept getting dark and darker. And one day, I just decided, I'd had enough. I thought it was a strong decision. For me. "

"So, what happened?" I gently encourage her after she goes quiet, lost in her own memories for a moment.

"Nothing. I came out for dinner, listened to my mum try to make conversation with me, trying so hard, just to make me smile. And I realized I couldn't do it to her. That until I could live for myself again, I'd live for her. Just that realization, it made me smile. Really smile, for the first time in months. And the relief in her face in that moment, changed everything for me. I will never ever say it will work for everyone. But it did for me. Every person's story is different, but that is mine."

She leans forward from the headboard and reaches for my hands. I grab hers as fast as I can, squeezing them, and she almost chuckles.

"Hey, it wasn't the last time I contemplated it. But things got better, in tiny increments, every day. And it got to the point where I could consider going back to school. And I did. I got all my things together, told myself I could turn back any time. That first day back, I walked into my dorm and a crazy hippie brunette was lying under the bed, her two mismatched socked feet sticking out while she rummaged around under there for something. She was my first and almost only friend for a long time."

"Nutso?" I can only imagine it would be her.

"Ha, yes, the one and only. Sarah."

"What happened with Brent?" I try to ask lightly, hoping the answer involves a firing squad or a pit of live alligators.

"Nothing. Through some lawyer friend's help, we got the websites to take down the video, but we couldn't get those emails back and they were either ignored or forgotten by then. Brent skipped town, no one could find him. And I... I just didn't want to waste any more of my life on him."

"And you? What happened with you?" I want to hear her claim her victory, her success, her achievement of having survived.

"I'm here." She smiles. It's small but incandescent.

I pull her into my lap and she kisses me and it's sweet like burnt caramel.

"I'm here, too. With you. And there's nowhere else I'd rather be."

***

Her breath is slowing down and her body retracts into a relaxed, little ball, curled up against me. Her bare shoulder, still slightly glistening with sweat, presses up against my face and I turn just a little to drop my lips in a kiss on her warm skin. She's sweet and salty all at once. I run my tongue over my mouth to lick up every little molecule of her scent. Even now, just moments after completely giving into her, I can feel my core inflamed at the thought of being inside her again. Feeling her engulf my hardness, milking me and coaxing me to give myself all to her.

"Cadence?"

"Hmmm?" she mumbles, probably barely a breath from sleep.

"You're sexy."

She giggles a little at my childish compliment.

"Thanks?"

"What? You are."

"You're pretty sexy too there, Mr. Musician." She turns in my arms and I'm staring down at her face, stroking the bangs falling over her eyes to the side.

She is the sight of absolute perfection. I lean over and graze the tip of her nose with my lips.

"Yeah? Well, guess what?"

She just smiles, a dimple flashing for a moment on her left cheek.

"You're my muse," I confess to her.

Her eyes close, her eyelashes fluttering like little brown feathers against her pale cheek, before she opens them and stares up at me.

"You're my music," she confesses back.

And it's in that moment, I know my heart is lost to her forever.

Chapter Twenty-One

CADENCE

It's bright. Someone's turned the light on in the world and I'm not happy about it.

I make that unhappiness known in the way of kicking my legs and grabbing the sheets and rolling around on the bed until the sheet and I are the perfect shape of a human burrito.

"Up and at 'em, Mary!" an obnoxious voice is saying. And an obnoxious hand is grabbing my burrito wrap and trying to unroll me from the comfort of my burrito cocoon.

But my feet are quick and very defensive of my right to sleep in. They kick out and I feel them connect with something.

Something boney.

Something that is now as unhappy as I am.

"Ow! You kicked me." That something is astute.

"Good. And I'll do it again if you don't leave me alone," I threaten.

The room goes quiet and I'm glad that my words have been taken in the way they were intended, seriously.

Then suddenly I feel an entire obnoxious body fling itself onto the bed on top of me and it's digging its fingers into my sides and even through the burrito wrap I can't help but succumb to the relentless tickling, screaming at the top of my lungs for help as my attacker takes advantage of my weakness and unwraps me from my cotton sanctuary.

"I freed you! You're welcome," my attacker not-freer throws his hands up in the air in a misguided sense of victory.

I wonder, not for the first time, just how much it really hurts when you kick a man in the balls. Even in my morning grump, I feel that may be cutting my nose off to spite my face so I leave it for another time.

"Why are you not letting me sleep? My beauty, ergo, your attraction to me, counts on it!" I grumble at Sebastian.

He falls back onto the bed next to me and pulls my head to his chest, stroking my hair, knowing already that that's my weakness.

"Shhhh, it's breakfast time. The neighbors came by and asked if we want to walk to the restaurant with them since they're leaving today too."

"Tell 'em 'sure', you'll go with them, and I'll stay here sleeping. Bye."

"Well, yes, that's an option, but instead, I told them you were getting ready and we'll meet them in fifteen minutes. That was ten minutes ago."

"Fine, wake me up in four minutes."

"But then I won't have time to give you an orgasm."

"You don't anyway." I poke my tongue out at him.

"Challenge accepted!"

***

"Hmm, I guess I did have enough time after all," Sebastian snickers as we step off our patio and onto the walkway up to the main building. I elbow him as I wave at the two people walking up to us.

We introduce ourselves to the older couple and together we make our way to the restaurant.

"So, you guys are leaving today as well?" Linda, the wife, a stunning blonde, asks me once the waiter's taken our order.

"Yes," I nod, pouting slightly at the reminder. Reality is waiting for us and who knows what else.

"You know, you just look so familiar to me, I just cannot place your face," her husband, Greg, says to Sebastian, who just grins and shrugs.

"Have you had a good time?" I ask them, hoping to distract Greg.

"Hmm-hmm," Linda nods, taking a sip of her mimosa, "Amazing. We're already sorry to leave. We go back to the US today."

"Oh, where are you from?" Although I'm pretty sure I can already guess from their accents.

"Oh, we're from Texas." Linda smiles at me, with a tinge of homesickness.

"I'VE GOT IT!" Greg roars suddenly, the three of us jump out of our seats.

"You're from that band...that string band that won the Grammy this year." Greg shouts, pointing at Sebastian, who is now trying to hide behind his menu.

"Honey...I don't think..." Linda starts to say, trying to calm her husband down.

"It IS him, I swear!" Greg roars again, and I just shrug at Sebastian who puts down his menu.

"I'm so sorry, he gets really fixated on things until he can figure it out," Linda apologizes for her husband who still hasn't stopped staring at Sebastian.

"I changed my mind, let's go back to our room and have sex," Sebastian leans over and whispers into my ear. I swat him away and give him my biggest smile, "So, honey, why don't you tell Greg here, what it's like to be a Grammy winner?"

Greg slams his hand onto the table and lets out a big belly laugh, "I told you it was him! How are you doing, pal?" He reaches over the table and grabs Sebastian's hand, shaking it up and down until I think Sebastian's arm is about to be pulled from its socket.

The customers at the other tables are starting to stare at us, and it's not until Linda physically extracts her husband's hand from Sebastian's that he finally lets go and sits back down.

"You guys are awesome!" Greg bellows across the table to Sebastian. "Man, I'm not much for classical music, but the way you guys mix it with some good ol' classic rock n roll, we love it! Don't we honey?!"

Sebastian, used to the attention, just smiles and lets Greg continue to shower him with praise, nodding and eating his food, but never really adding anything to what Greg's saying.

"So, what are you guys doing here? Tell me you eloped, that would be such a romantic story." Linda asks us, when she finally has a chance to get a word in while Greg takes a big forkful of eggs.

"Well, actually," Sebastian grins at me, and I wonder what's going on in his mind, "We DID just get married last night," he leans over and whispers to Linda, whose eyes grow wide.

"Oh my gosh!!!! Did you hear that honey, they're MARRIED!" She yells, and I suddenly see the resemblance between the two.

I turn and just stare at Sebastian, who winks and goes back to his food, as if nothing has happened.

"How did it happen? Tell us, tell us, tell us!" The blonde jumps out of her seat with excitement, flinging her fork to the floor.

"Yes, Muffinbottom, why don't you tell them?" Sebastian says to me, a look of innocence on his face.

I glare at him, and turn back to our breakfast partners.

"Well, actually, Sebastian has been in love with me FOR YEARS. But I was never interested in him at all. I didn't find him very…how do I say this…able to satisfy me in bed, you know." I wink at Linda conspiratorially, and her eyes grow wider as she leans in further across the table.

Sebastian elbows me and I turn and shoot him my brightest smile. He cocks his eyebrow and I can see the thoughts churning in his brain. This is going to get nasty.

"Now, now, don't be telling lies, Pinkywinky, you know that you were the one who was chasing me. Sending me all sorts of suggestive notes and…let's just say, undergarments that had not been through the wash yet."

The bastard.

"Well, Thumbdoodle, that was only after we had gotten together, you know, after your operation." I nod for emphasis.

"Operation?" both Greg and Linda ask, forks forgotten, hovering halfway to their mouths.

"Well, yes, we don't like to talk about it, but you guys won't tell anyone, will you?"

They shake their heads even as the drool collects in the corner of their mouths.

"Well, my Applewafflekins here," I say, leaning in with a pause, before whispering, "had a third testicle."

Next to me I hear Sebastian choke, spitting out his drink. I reach over and pat him gently on the back.

"Are you okay, Snickerpie?" I ask, my voice dripping with honey.

"Oh, um, yes, just fine. I just didn't realize that this drink had alcohol in it. You know, you shouldn't be drinking alcohol, Waffletoes."

I shake my head, this has gone too far, abort, abort, I beg him with my eyes.

"Why can't she have alcohol?" Greg asks, his ass barely touching his seat.

"Well, she's pregnant, of course."

"OHMYGOD!!! CONGRATULATIONS!" Linda shrieks.

"Oh no, it's not mine." Sebastian waves his hands in front of us. And I brace myself for what's coming. "It's her cousin's, I mean, her ex-lover's. But he left her for his next-door neighbor's dog walker, so that's why we got married. I'm gonna take care of this little lady and her three babies."

And he reaches over and pat me, my stomach specifically, and my ex-lover cousin's unborn triplet babies.

The two sets of eyes across the table finally blink after a few seconds and turn towards each other, jaws barely clearing the table.

We take this moment to run.

"Oohh, um, honey, I don't feel so well," I moan, kicking Sebastian under the table.

"Oh, her morning sickness has been terrible, I better take her back to her room. You two enjoy the breakfast now, it's on me! Enjoy the rest of your trip."

I jump out of my chair and try not to run out of the hotel restaurant, careful not to drop the imaginary fetuses, pushing open the entrance doors and turning the corner just in time to let out the giant guffaw I'd been holding in.

Sebastian catches up with me, his hands covering his mouth and I'm wondering how he can hold his laughter in. He's shaking his head and he just keeps running back to our villa. He disappears down the walkway and about ten second later I hear a roar of laughter.

The sound of him laughing sets me off again and I bend over at the hip, trying to breathe between my laughter. It's a good five minutes before I can just barely make my way back to our room.

SEBASTIAN

"Ready to go?" I nudge her with my toe.

"No," she mumbles, her face still buried in the cushion.

"Well, we have no choice," I remind her.

"Sure, we do. We can stay. We can go live with that kangaroo family. We can take turns sleeping in her front bag."

I kneel down and gently stroke her hair. She purrs and it sends shivers through my body.

"It's time to go, baby."

"Don't YOU want to stay?"

"More than you know. But not more than I want to go back to our lives...so I can show you off."

She pauses and then sighs, heaving herself off the couch.

"Sweet talker." She raises herself up on her tiptoes and presses a soft kiss to my lips. "We're really going back to our lives together?"

"Yes, of course," I tell her.

"I mean, going back together, as in, when we go back there, we'll be together."

"As opposed to..."

"Not being together," she explains, but clarifying nothing.

"Right. What?"

"This is not...just for here?" she asks, her voice suddenly filled with insecurity.

I thread my fingers through hers and tell her with more conviction than I have ever said anything, "No, it's for here, there, everywhere and in between."

And I can see she likes the thought of that.

***

"Over here! Seb! Cadence!"

Over the bobbing heads all going in the direction of baggage claim, I can see Hank waving to us, and I wave back and lead Cadence over to him.

"Fucking hell! All hell is breaking loose! Quick, we better get you guys to the car!"

Cadence looks over at me, and I just shrug. I have as little idea about what's going on as she has.

One of the SUVs is waiting for us at the pick-up point and I help Cadence get in first, and slide in after her. Hanks throws our bags into the trunk and climbs into the passenger seat.

"Take us back to the hotel, please," he tells the driver and then turns to us.

"What's going on?" we ask him.

"Come on! Like you don't know."

"We don't. Hello, the only contact we've had with the outside world is my call to you to come pick us up."

"So, you don't have something to tell me? About you two?"

"Well, um, I mean..."

Cadence looks over at me. We'd agreed that we wouldn't be making a big announcement. If one of the guys asked then we'd confirm that we were together, but for now, we'd hoped that we could fly under the radar. Of course, disappearing for three days together was going to get some tongues wagging.

"Just spit it out, Hank."

"No way, this is Dennis' territory, I'm just here to pick you up." He turns and slides his earphones into his ears and tries to ignore us.

***

"What the hell have you done?" Dennis yells at us as soon as we walk through the rehearsal room door. His face is red and it looks like he's spent the last three hours running his fingers through his hair trying not to pull it all out.

"It's good to see you too, Dennis! We missed you!" I reply and turn to wink at Cadence.

"No, no, no, there will be none of that." He points at me, "You! Sit there." He points at the sofa. "And Cadence. You." He turns and points to the recliner opposite the couch. "You sit there."

"Yes, Dad." We move to sit in our respective assigned seats.

"Now, answer me this time. What the hell have you done?"

"What are you talking about, Dennis?"

"You disappear for three days...TOGETHER! And this morning, I get a Google alert to say that, and I QUOTE, "Sebastian Dupont from Grammy Winner Band Elopes with Oz High School Music Teacher!" He turns to us, his mouth dropping open.

Cadence drops her head, her hair falling in front of her face, a move I've become accustomed to now, when she wants to hide her expression. Her shaking shoulders however are giving her away.

"Oh." I shrug, "That. That's nothing." I get up from my seat, "Anyone want a coffee?"

Dennis roars, "Sit your fucking ass down!"

I sink back down into my seat and bite the inside of my cheek trying not to laugh. "Chill, man."

"I will chill, when you tell me what the hell's going on! Are you two married?"

"No, of course not, you psycho!" I yell back at him. "We just went away for a few days!"

Dennis takes a deep breath, almost dizzy with relief and sits down in the empty seat next to me. "Then where did the rumor come from?"

"Dude, are you NEW? How many times have they come up with all sorts of shit?"

"Yeah, but this one...I mean, they mentioned Cadence. Not some random celebrity."

"Um, yeah, well, lucky guess." I shrug, biting the inside of my cheek. If Dennis knew I was the source of the rumor, he'd castrate me with a rusty knife.

"So...you're not married?" he confirms.

"No."

"okay. Yeah, okay, great."

"Wait, hang on why? What if we WERE married? It's going to happen to one of us at some point, ya know."

"Then I'd want the story broken my way."

"Fine. But you should know, while we're not married, we are...together."

"Well, yeah," his face utters the silent 'duh'.

"What do you mean, 'well, yeah'?"

"I mean, well, we had a freaking pool going, for fuck's sake, to see how long it would take you two to get your acts together."

"Who won?" Cadence finally speaks up.

"None of your business."

"So, what are we going to do about these marriage rumors then?"

"What we always do, ignore them." He gets up and goes over to his laptop, his shoulders relaxed.

"You sure?"

"I guess, there was some other weird shit in the article as well, some stuff about you having some operation and just marrying Cadence to take care of her unborn babies."

"Er, yeah, that is bloody weird," I say as I get up and sit down next to Cadence, throwing my arm around her shoulders.

The door flings open and the band walks in, carrying take-out and drinks.

"MR. and MRS. Dupont! You are back!!" Marius bellows, walking into the room with his arms outstretched. "Can't wait to babysit your bastard kids!"

"Oh, for god's sake. I'm outta here." Dennis moves towards the doorway, then stops, "Guys, what do you think, our concert next Friday, if we get Cadence up on stage for a song? I mean, the concert is mainly to launch the new band name and to test out some of the new songs, but a teaser for the piano pieces might be good."

Brad shrugs and balances his bow on top of his head, "Fine by me, get the audience excited for our new album."

"Guys, I don't want to be stepping on any toes. You, um, hired me for the album, not any concerts. Maybe you want to keep performances for yourselves and just put me on playback or something." Cadence offers thoughtfully.

"Are you kidding? You're going to be a hit." Marius smiles at her, and I'm grateful that they love her almost as much as I do.

"What should we play?" Jez throws out for discussion.

"I've got just the song."

Chapter Twenty-Two

CADENCE

I don't ever want this moment to end.

I can't breathe deep and fast enough, I need more and more oxygen to fuel my eyes, my ears, my brain, to process it all, to imprint it in my memory forever.

The noise is deafening. Literally. I feel like it's overloaded my eardrums and everything is just white noise now, or silence, I can't differentiate it. I'm too busy looking out into the crowd and feeling the vibrations of their applause hum through every cell of my body.

The lights lash over my eyes and I'm turning to my left. Sebastian is grinning at me, his face glistening with sweat as he winks at me, holding out an upturned thumb.

"Yay, Cadence!" I can just make out a voice screaming, and I think it's Marius to my right.

And then the crowd starts to chant, "Cadence! Cadence! Cadence!" and it's taking me some time before I realize that's my name.

"I think we can convince our guest to stay for one more song, what do you think, guys?" I hear Sebastian yell into the microphone, his voice slightly distorted.

The chants explode and suddenly, I hear the opening notes to The Verve's "Bitter Sweet Symphony". I turn back to the piano and let the music sing through me.

The song comes to a close and the audience drowns out the epic ending with their screaming.

I stand up, wanting to feel the power of their applause wash over me. I see Sebastian put down his cello and walk over to me. He stops for a moment and holds out his hands in the sign of a love heart to the audience. Then he turns to me, he pulls me into his arms and bends me over into a deep, deep kiss.

I don't ever want this moment to end.

***

"You were sensational," Sebastian whispers into my ear as we go backstage, the sound of the crowd trailing us as the lights come up. His arms come up behind me as he grazes his lips against my neck. I shiver under his touch even though my body is burning from the heat of the spotlights and the adrenaline of performing.

"YOU were phenomenal," I turn in his arms and kiss him hard, tasting the gentle saltiness of the sweat on his lips.

"What about us?" Marius and Jez butt in, wrapping their arms around us in a big group hug, pressing me even harder against Sebastian.

"Eh, so-so," I shrug nonchalantly and wink at Sebastian.

"Titbitchums!" Marius curses at me and pokes me in the side, making me yelp. "I was the star."

I giggle and wriggle out of Sebastian's hold to give Marius a big hug. "Yes, you were. You were bloody brilliant."

Marius huffs, "You're just saying that because...I was."

I laugh and give him a kiss on the cheek.

"Oi," I feel myself pulled back against Sebastian's chest. "Get off my woman," he growls at Marius.

"Oh, relax. I've been trying to get YOU on your woman for weeks now. Made me lose the damn pool," Marius grumbles and wanders off down the hall to the catering area. The rest follow him and the hallway starts to empty as the crew gets to work packing up the stage.

"Back to you. My angel muse," Sebastian murmurs low and dark against my ear. The hairs on the back of my neck prickle and my nipples twinge. He grinds against me and I can feel he's hard. I push back against him, and he growls. "Do you think the crowd would like it more or less if next time in the middle of a song, I just bend you right over the piano and take you then and there?"

The image instantly plays out in my mind, and I pull his arms tighter around me, as I can't help but notice a pulsing between my legs.

"Well, I guess that all depends on whether it affects our playing or not?" I rasp, his teeth grazing against my shoulder.

"It might, but it would give them something else to focus on."

"I'm not sure I want 10,000 women focusing on your cock," I turn and whisper into his ear. His hips instantly thrust against me.

"Say it again, that last word."

"You mean, you like it when I say 'cock'?"

"Fuck. You are going to kill me."

He grabs my hand and drags me down the hallway.

"What are you doing?"

"Trust me, in a minute you're not going to have to ask."

He stops at a door, an empty room we used as the greenroom before the concert.

Yanking the door open, he peeks inside, and asks, "Anyone in here?"

The light's on but it looks empty. Grinning to me, he pushes me in and flicks off the light as he closes the door. There's a soft hue from the adjoining bathroom's mirror light and my eyes are just starting adjust as he presses me up against the closed door.

"Say it again."

"What, baby?" I run my fingernails over his scalp and feel him shiver.

"You know."

I pull his head down to mine, kissing him hard, as his hands come around to slide under my skirt, his fingers hooking into my panties and pulling them down my legs. Tearing my mouth off his, I give him what he wants.

"I. Want. Your. Cock," I growl the words into his ear, one by one. He hisses and in one movement tucks his hands under my ass and lifts me up, wrapping my legs around him and pinning me against the door.

"Again," he commands me.

"Your cock belongs inside me." I obey. My legs squeeze, pulling him closer, and I feel him reach in to slide his zipper down.

"Yes, yes, it does, babygirl." He snarls against my throat, his voice thick with want.

I can already feel how my body is getting ready for him, the slickness between my legs growing with every second. I want him so much I can barely breathe.

"One more time," he struggles to say and I almost bite my tongue as I feel his hardness press against me.

"Give me your cock, Sebastian!" I beg him, pushing my hips away from the door, trying to push down on him.

"Your wish is my command." He growls and pins my body hard against the door, thrusting his hips and sliding his entire, thick, hard length inside me.

I'm burning, his thickness stretching me as I drag some air into my lungs.

I'm completely lost, I can feel his body against me, rocking back and forth, and him entering me over and over. I give myself completely to him. And let him take everything from me.

"Yes, yes, yes, God fucking yes, Sebastian. I'll say 'cock' a hundred times a day if you'll keep fucking me like this."

I can just make out a soft chuckle in between his heavy breaths. "I'm so close, baby, I've been dying to be inside you all night."

I'm teetering on the edge, each time he slams into me, I inch a bit closer. His hardness growing even now, more and more with every time he drives himself deeper into me, grazing against the slick, pulsing walls of my sex. My mind and body are screaming for release.

His mouth moves down and he bites my nipples through my shirt. That's all I can take.

"Fuck!!!!!!" I scream, and my whole body is wracked over and over with waves of orgasm. It gets better every time with him. My nails score lines down his back and he grunts in both pain and the effort of holding me, keeping himself buried deep in of me even as I'm shaking in his arms.

I try to lock my gaze with his, and whisper, "Come for me, with your cock in me."

The words make his eyes glaze over and he digs his hands around my waist and pulls me down one last time onto him as he thrusts into me.

"Oh god." The breath gurgles in his throat, and his body jerks between my legs. I pull him tighter against me, and he groans again, his hands digging hard into my ass as he empties himself into me. I hold him as the tremors of the aftermath rock through him, and his body starts to relax its tension.

"Fuck." He whispers, and he lets go of my legs and we both fall to the floor.

I'm straddling him, my legs on either side of him, the tip of his softening cock still pressed up against me. I move down so my head can rest on his chest. It rises and falls high and low, high and low, as he tries to steady his breathing.

"Damn, girl. If we keep doing this, I'm going to have some weird Pavlovian response to performing," he whispers breathlessly.

"If you promise we do this before each concert, I'm going to have to go on tour with you."

His arms instantly come around to hug me tight to him. "It's a deal."

I smile, but just for a moment, before I realize, this is all soon going to have to come to an end. Our lives are turning in very different directions...and locations.

"Come on, I'm parched," I say, struggling to my feet, as I reach for my panties and pull them on.

He watches me from his spot on the floor as I compose myself.

"Hey, come back here," he says holding his hand out to me.

I take it and kneel down next to him. He looks up at me, and even in the dark, his pupils are tender and kind. It's a look I know is reserved just for me.

"I'm serious. Come on tour with us."

"I can't."

"Why not? You want to clear it with the guys? They'll be just as rapt as I am. Didn't you hear the crowd tonight?"

"No. It's just, I can't. It's not my life. It's yours."

"Let's make it ours." He insists gently.

I smile at him. I don't want to talk about this now, think about this now. I just want to enjoy it.

I get back on my feet and drag him up. "Come on, we can talk about this later. Right now, I think you should buy your runaway success guest artist a drink!"

I watch as he straightens his clothes, his eyes still on me. The truth is, every part of me wants to say yes. Every part but my brain. My brain that knows that it's just not meant to be.

"Okay, temptress, drinks are on me!" he opens the door and steps out, holding it open for me.

Just as I follow him out, I swear I hear a voice coming from deep in the room, maybe the bathroom. I turn back into the room, this time there's a distinct, 'Shhhhh'.

I step towards the noise to go check it out, just as Sebastian grabs my hand and drags me away, "Come on, slowpoke! Drinks are only free for another ten minutes!"

I turn back to see if anyone's following us.

There isn't.

But I know there was someone there.

And I swear it was a female voice.

Chapter Twenty-Three

CADENCE

"Get up, guys, get up," a male voice is calling us. And it's suddenly bright.

I grab the sheet and pull it over my head. I can hear Sebastian growling his own disgust at being woken so early after the night we had.

"Cadence. Sebastian. Guys, wake up, we need to talk to you." I think it's Jez, but I know there's more than one person in the room.

"Later," Sebastian growls.

"No. Now." Dennis' voice speaks up. That seems to get Sebastian's attention. He sighs and sits up.

I hear the crinkle of newspaper and then silence.

Sebastian mumbles something and I hear everyone leave.

"Yay, back to sleep," I gurgle happily and tuck the sheet back under my chin.

"Cadence. You need to get up." Sebastian says, and his voice is firm. Enough for it to penetrate my sleepy haze.

I turn around and he's sitting up, looking at the newspaper in his hand.

"What's going on? I was looking forward to a sleep-in. It's the right of a teacher during school holiday time." I grumble, rubbing my eyes, waiting for them to focus.

"I know, baby, I know. But um, something's happened."

"What?"

"Look. Um. We'll take it care of it, but it looks like..." his voice peters off, and I notice he's still gripping the newspaper in his hand.

"Give me the newspaper, Sebastian."

"Wait. Let me..." he starts and then fades out again. It must be bad if he can't even tell me.

"Just give it to me."

He sighs and hands it me.

There, on the front page of the paper is a half-page picture of me. Of me having sex with Sebastian.

And the words, "Rockstar's Sex-Crazed New Wife- Ex Porn Star?"

My eyes drift to the row of pictures below the main one, and my blood freezes in my veins.

"Oh my God." It's a collage of the pictures from the sex video leaked of me seven years ago.

"Oh my god, oh my god, oh my god." I can't believe what I'm seeing. After all this time, back on the front page of the newspaper. "Oh my god, Sebastian!!!"

Sebastian rips the paper away from me and throws it over the side of the bed. He turns back and all I can do is stare at him. My mind is completely frozen. I can't even comprehend what has just happened.

"Cadence," Sebastian starts, reaching out to touch me.

I can't help but pull away, jumping out of the bed.

"Oh my god, oh my god, oh my god."

Sebastian comes up and wraps his arms around me, trying to hold me, stop me from pacing.

"It's okay, we're going to take care of it, it's going to be okay."

But it's not.

Because I've been here before.

I know how bad it was.

I know how bad it's going to get.

It's not something I can ever get through again.

And then the dam breaks, and I feel my eyes fill with tears, tears that fall and never, ever stop.

I feel his arms around me, but they do nothing.

I hear his words calming me, but they do nothing.

I feel his promises that everything is going to be all right, but they do nothing.

Because nothing can turn back time.

SEBASTIAN

Her sobs are the most horrifying sounds I've ever heard.

Because they remind me of my helplessness and her hopelessness.

They tell me that I can do nothing.

They tell me that this pain that she's feeling, is hers and hers alone, and I can want to carry it for her as much as I want, but not until she's ready, is it going to go away.

It's been three hours since the guys brought the newspaper in, and she's barely stopped crying for a moment. Sometimes, her sobs will fade to a whimper, and I think she's fallen asleep, but then the cycle starts again.

I haven't even had a chance to think about how this has happened, and who's responsible for it.

At this moment, I'm still just trying to figure out how to get Cadence through it minute by minute.

She hasn't moved from this ball that she curled into when she finally let me lay her back down onto the bed.

And she hasn't said another word since she first saw the pictures.

These pictures of a most private and intimate moment between a man and woman.

Between her and me. And between her and him.

The pain and humiliation of seven years ago is now dragged to the present. I can't even imagine what is going through her head right now.

There's a gentle knock on the door and I ignore it. She doesn't want to see anyone right now, and I'm not so sure I want to see anyone either.

A minute passes and there's another knock.

I sigh and get off the bed and open the door a small crack.

It's Sarah.

"Let me see her."

"I don't think..."

"I've been here before with her, let me in," Sarah says softly but firmly.

I nod and open the door wider and she steps quietly into the room.

I watch as she slips off her shoes and crawls onto the bed, wrapping her arms around Cadence.

"Hey, sweetie, it's me. I'm here," she whispers, and I see Cadence let herself be pulled into her friend's arms.

"Can we have a few minutes? Please?" Sarah says to me, and I hesitate, but then leave, closing the door behind me.

The guys are all sitting in the living area, facing the TV with the sound off.

"How's she doing?" Marius asks, his face worried.

"Not great," I say, sinking into the couch, rubbing my hands over my face, exhausted. "We know anything yet?"

"Dennis hasn't gotten back yet. I'm sure he'll get to the bottom of it."

The room goes quiet and I strain to listen for voices coming from the bedroom.

"Hey," Jez says softly as he comes over and sits on the arm of the chair. "You okay?"

I just shrug. I haven't even begun to sort through my own feelings yet.

"Did you...um, did you know? About the...?" Jez voice fades away as he tries to find the right word.

"The what?"

"The pictures."

"How the fuck was I supposed to know, unless I set up a camera myself...are you fucking suggesting...?" I snap at him, irritated.

"Whoa, calm down, mate. No, I didn't mean the ones of you and Cadence, I meant the ones from before."

"Oh, sorry. I'm just, I'm a little on edge." I lower my voice, immediately feeling bad for attacking my friend.

"It's okay."

"Um, yeah, yeah, I knew. She told me about them when we were away. But I don't think...I don't think she thought it was ever going to come up again."

I push myself out of my seat and stare out the window.

The sky is a flat, dull grey. Lifeless. Not a hint of sunlight or storm. Just like the clouds have died and nothing but their shells are left, spreading out like a canvas of grey cells over the horizon.

I replay her voice in my head, telling me how she had suffered the last time the videos had come out. Where it had taken her, how it had affected her life.

How much pain and humiliation it had brought her. And now it was all back. Two-fold. And I was the cause. This wouldn't have happened if she wasn't with me. I know it and she knows it. So much for promising to protect her after the club incident, I couldn't even shield her from attacks in our own space.

"Fuck!" The anger suddenly hits me and I slam my fist into the window. The glass holds under my attack, but not without shuddering for a moment, and I shake my wrist, the shock having been sent back up my knuckles and into my body.

"Sebastian." I look over and see Sarah stepping out of the room, closing the door behind her. "I'll be in the hallway waiting. Call me when she's ready to leave."

"Leave?" I feel the blood drain from my face. I run over to her. "What do you mean?"

"I think you should just go in and talk to her. I'll be right outside." Her voice is kind but strong. I wonder what they've talked about since I left the room.

I take a breath, steeling myself and open the door to the bedroom.

She's standing with her back to me, staring out the window in the same stance I was in just seconds ago.

"Cadence. How are you doing, babe?" I ask her. Waiting for her to turn to face me.

She doesn't.

"I'm...I'm gonna go. Sarah's waiting for me. But I just ...I wanted to say good bye first." Her hand comes up to press against her mouth.

I don't know what I'm hearing. I shake my head to clear the buzz in my ears.

"What...what are you talking about, where are you going?" I stutter, hardly able to get the words out, not wanting to make them real.

She finally spins on her feet to look at me and her face breaks my heart. The light in her eyes is gone, and those normally vibrant eyes are sunken into her face, her cheeks are pale and gaunt. It's as if he life in her has just died, in the space of a few hours.

"I have to get away from here." I can't tell if she's telling me or begging me.

"No, stay here, I can...I can protect you here." *Don't leave me*, I swallow the silent words.

"No, you can't. It's too late. It's done." And I know she's right. I can't take it back. If I had the power to collect up every printed newspaper, every digital imprint of those pictures of her, I would. I would crawl on my hands and knees to get it done. But it just can't be. And she knows it.

"But I can help you from here on out. We can face it together."

"You don't get it, do you?" She looks up, and it's almost as if she's looking right through me.

"Tell me, what don't I get?" I don't know how to help her, and it's tearing me up inside.

"It's not the same for you as it is for me. One picture ONE time...is one thing. Now they have TWO. Do you know what TWO pictures is, Sebastian? Do you know what that means? To the world, it means I'm a SLUT!"

She yells the word and all the pain she's feeling is carried in that one word.

"Did you READ what they said in the article, Sebastian? They didn't call YOU a porn star, did they? It doesn't matter that sex requires TWO people. But no, it's just me. Because not once, but TWICE, I've been caught fucking some guy on camera and it's out for the WHOLE FUCKING WORLD TO SEE."

She's pacing around the room now. Her hands a wringing and her face is scrunched up, all I can sense from her is restlessness, frustration, agitation. And all I can do is stand there and watch. I can't reach out to her, because she doesn't want me to. Because she thinks I don't understand. And, how can I? She's right. The world is going to judge her so much crueler for this than they will me.

"Do you know how old I was when that first video came out? I was eighteen. And it was of me making love to my boyfriend. Eight years later, again, it was of me making love to someone I thought was the love of my life. No men in between. That last eight years could just be a giant whorefest for me for all they can guess."

"Who cares?" I throw my hands up, hoping to lighten the situation.

She whips her head around and I can see the last vestiges of blood drain from her face. She knows now I don't understand.

"I CARE! I'm a TEACHER, Sebastian! What I do MATTERS. Every decision I've made for the last five years is to protect me and to protect my kids. How can I face them now, how can I face anyone at the school now? But you don't get it - hell this is probably going to boost YOUR rock star reputation."

"Hang on..." I walk up to her. This can't still be how she thinks of me.

"This affects me, the life I live. Maybe you've lived too long in your bubble to know that most people aren't afforded the same consideration you are. You have a story run about you eloping and having a third testicle, and most people think it's funny. Well, I can tell you this isn't funny."

"Wait," I grab her arm and swing her around to face me. "Why are you mad at me?"

She sighs and for the first time looks me directly eyes. I have to bite back the need to kiss her pain and anger away. This can't be solved with sex.

"I'm not." She sighs again, the air deflating her lungs and her body grows even smaller. "I'm not mad at you. This isn't your fault...but, it wouldn't have happened without you. Can you see the difference?"

I do. I know. And I don't know how to tell her I can't change it.

"Who do you think did this, Sebastian?" she asks suddenly.

"I don't know, we're trying to find out." I tell her honestly.

"You won't. Because even if Dennis does, I don't think you'll ever know about it."

"What are you talking about?"

"It was Hailey," she says. And my heart drops. I can't argue about this with her again.

"Cadence."

"Stop." She puts her hand up.

"What?"

"Stop, I don't want to hear you defend her. Not now. Not over this."

"There's no way...no reason she would do this."

"She was there, Sebastian, she was there! Last night, in the greenroom! I heard her just as we were leaving!"

"Why didn't you say anything?"

"I didn't think she was going to do anything! I thought she'd just gotten stuck in there and hadn't wanted to bother us. Fuck, was I wrong."

"Even if she was, she wouldn't have done this, and how would she have known about the videos of you from before?" I don't have any other way to argue this except with reason. But I know Cadence's insistence has reached a level beyond that now.

"I don't know. I just know... that she was jealous of me being with you because she wanted you... that she was the only one other than us in that room last night... and now there are pictures of us FUCKING on the front fucking page. And all you can do is say, it wasn't her."

I don't know what to say. I know without a shadow of a doubt that Hailey has no feelings for me but I can't explain it to Cadence.

"Trust me, please, you've got to trust me. It wasn't her." I reach out to touch her face and she pulls away, her eyes filled with hurt. And I feel something snap between us. Something break.

She walks to her side of the bed and picks up her bag. Then as if there's no energy left in her body, she sits down on the bed.

"Don't go. We can't work it out unless we're together. Don't give up on us." I beg her softly. I can't believe this is happening.

"There is no us. I'm sorry, Sebastian. I'm so sorry. I just, I can't do this again. I can't handle this level of scrutiny, this absolute loss of privacy. But...it's not even that. You say you want to protect me, but you don't even trust me enough to consider what I'm saying about Hailey. Or you won't explain why. What's the point in protecting me if you don't even trust me?"

"I do trust you, but you have to trust me. I can't tell you why, I just, I just know it's not her."

"You won't even consider it? You won't even ask her?"

I can't lie to her. I'll keep her here by restraint, by force, before I keep her here by deception. So I just shake my head. By form of answer. By form of disbelief of what's about to happened.

"Ok," she relents. "Then I have to go."

She stands up and runs to the door but I jump over the bed and slam my back against it before she can get there. She stops in front of me, refusing to look at me.

"Cadence." I cradle her face in my palm. "Oh baby, my Cadence." I pull her against my chest and she doesn't fight me.

Her body breaks into sobs and I feel the tears start to stream down my cheeks. I want to tell her to take me with her, that I can leave all this behind. But the fear that she'll say no stops me.

"I have to go, Sebastian," she whispers when her sobs finally die down.

I bury my face in her hair, breathing in those orange blossoms one last time, before stepping away from the door.

"You might be walking out that door, but don't forget, you're still my here, there, everywhere and in between." I tell her.

"And you'll always be mine."

Chapter Twenty-Four

CADENCE

There are moments in your life that you wish you could relive; some where you'd do things completely differently, and some just to do the exact the same thing again. And again. And again.

I can't decide which way I would go with my moments with Sebastian.

Would I have just let him reach for the rosin, shrugged and walked out of his life forever?

Would I have never taken the $50 000 deal?

Would I have not let him kiss me that first time outside his hotel room door?

Would I have torn up the check when he showed up at the school, and never let him whisk me away?

I don't know.

I do know, that had I any other choice, I wouldn't have walked away from him. Because, without him, these last few days have been the worst torture I've ever endured.

I miss him so much that it hurts to think about him and it hurts even more not to. It had been so long since I'd let myself feel those feelings of intimacy and even sexual desire, when I'd let myself go with Sebastian, it was like everything was new. And it was the happiest I've ever been.

If I don't remember the smiles, the laughs, the kisses, the sharing of our secrets, does it mean it never happened?

Because right now, the only thing that's getting me through each minute, each hour, is to lose myself in those moments when I was in his arms, and nothing else in the world existed.

The question is, had it all been worth it?

The answer scares me, because it might tell me, that the only way to ever be happy again, to be back in his arms, is to risk everything.

"Cadence?" Sarah's voice pierces through my thoughts.

"Hmm?"

"Um, there's a call for you."

As always, I have to bite down the hope that it's Sebastian, even though I've asked her not to pass on any of his calls.

"Oh, thanks," I reach out for the phone, "Who is it?"

"It's Greg," she says, naming the high school principal. She looks grim and I wonder if he's said anything to her first.

"Hi, Greg," I say into the phone, trying to sound as upbeat as I can.

"Cadence. How are you?" He sounds genuinely concerned, and I can't imagine the position he's been put in.

"As well as you can expect."

"Ok, well, I hope it gets better soon. Unfortunately, I don't think this conversation's going to help."

My stomach sinks. I'm not sure what I had expected, but I had hoped that I at least had the support of the school after everything I'd done there.

"Ok."

"Look, the kids come back next week, we think it'd probably be less distracting for them if, at least for the first week, there's a substitute for your classes, just so they can get settled into their new term."

"And after?"

"And I guess, after, we're still discussing it."

"I didn't do anything wrong, Greg."

"I know, Cadence, if it was up to me, this wouldn't be a thing, and you'd be in your classroom where you belong, but...it's not just me."

"I understand."

"I'm doing everything I can, okay?"

"I know, I appreciate it,"

"Hey, take the week off to go somewhere, do something fun," he suggests.

"That's what got me in this position in the first place." I say, without a bit of irony.

I hear him sigh, I know he's in a hard place and I don't want to make it worse for him. "Take care, I'll talk to you soon."

Sarah's still there when I hang up the phone.

And she's there when the tears come again.

"Oh, honey," she comes around and wraps her arm around my shoulders. "It's not fair. It's not fair. But we're going to get through this. We have before, remember?"

I do remember. I remember being in this exact same position seven years ago.

And the wounds that I thought had long been scarred over, feel like they've been ripped open again.

SEBASTIAN

"Sebastian!" I hear my name yelled and I jerk into consciousness.

"Ahh, what?!" I snap.

"Geez, man, get your head out of the clouds. Didn't you hear us calling you?" Jez snaps back, irritated.

"No, I've blocked out your voices for the sake of my own sanity!"

"Dude. Chill." Brad intervenes, in his peacemaking way.

"Sorry, guys, um, was just daydreaming. What's up?"

"We were discussing the set list for next week. You up for it?"

"Yeah, er, whatever, you guys decide. Just let me know."

I push off my seat and wander over to the couch, letting my head fall back. It's pounding so hard, I can barely think. I've barely slept in days, and the endless rotation of vodka, then coffee and Red Bull hasn't been the helpful cocktail I'd hoped it would be.

Being cooped up in the hotel probably hasn't helped either.

Not that I know the difference.

I descended into my best impression of a zombie the moment Cadence walked out the door.

My heart twists just at the memory. Her face as she accused me of not caring about her, of not trusting her, of not protecting her.

And she was right. I hadn't protected her.

I'd been blindsided. Those pictures had shocked me just as much as her. And now, when I should be doing everything I can to protect her from the aftermath, it's too late, she won't let me.

And who can blame her.

It's almost four days later and I still don't know what happened.

I've broken every promise I've made to her, except one.

She will still always be my muse.

***

"Get up," a voice says just before a pillow comes down to smash over my head.

"Ferofffugturd!" I say, my voice muffled under the blanket.

"It's time, mate," another voice adds.

"For what?" I ask, pulling the blanket tighter around me and squeezing my eyes shut to block out the light.

"To live, mate. To live. And you know...shower."

I ignore them, hoping they'll go away if they realize I'm not up for this.

I should've known, I'm out of hopes this week.

"ARGHHHH FUCKKKKKNUCKLES! GET OFF MEEE!!" I yell as I feel the blanket pulled off me and two arms grab me by the legs and pull me off the bed.

"OOOMFFF!" I groan as I fall to the floor onto a pile of pillows.

"Leave me alone, cocksockers!" I growl at them, looking at the remaining three members of the band standing there chuckling at me.

"Dude. Seriously, we need to get out of here! We have serious cabin fever," Jez begs me, and scrunches up his nose looking around the room I've barely left in days.

"So, go. I'm not stopping you."

"All for one and one for all, right?" Marius remind me of our motto.

"I'm pretty sure we meant doing shots and having hangovers when we used to use that saying, bro." I cock an eyebrow at him.

He grins, "Maybe that's exactly what I meant."

Jez comes over and sits down on my legs.

"Say you'll get up and take a shower at least."

I try to kick him off but he holds on. He should've been a rodeo cowboy.

"Say you'll have a shower, stinky boy!"

"FINE!" I yell and he gets off me.

I take the chance to grab the blanket and try to pull it back over me.

"He's going in! CHARGE!" I hear Marius yell and suddenly an onslaught of hands are grabbing at me, pulling my t-shirt off and pulling me by the legs to my ensuite.

"Assault, assault!!!" I try to yell, as I feel the cold bathroom tile slide under my legs and back.

There's the sound of water as someone turns the shower on and suddenly, I'm cold and wet and half-naked in the shower with my three best friends in the world.

And I lose it. And I start to sob.

"Oh shit. We broke him." Brad stops and pulls back and points to me.

"I can't tell, is he REALLY crying or is it the shower?" Marius sticks his face in mine and stares at me.

"What do we do? WHAT DO WE DO?!" Jez freaks out and presses himself back against the shower wall.

And I don't stop. Sob after sob wracks through my body, even as my bandmates stand there and stare at me in horror.

"What the HELL is going on in here?"

We hear a fourth voice and turn around to see Dennis standing at the door.

"We, uh, we broke Sebastian," Jez confesses hanging his head.

"Oh geez, what did you do?" Dennis takes a step closer and I try to bite back the sobs, composing myself.

"We...we tried to get him to take a shower," Marius adds.

"They were just trying to help." I finally speak up. I grab Jez's hand and he helps me up. I smile at him, and even through the pain I'm feeling, my heart suddenly squeezes with love for these idiots standing here with me. Wet. In the shower.

Geez.

"Get the fuck out of here, pencilpricks, and let me get washed," I say, pushing them out of the bathroom.

They slosh out one by one.

"Hey," I call out just as they reach the bathroom door, "Thanks, guys."

They nod, and file out.

And I wonder if living on their love alone is going to be enough for me for the rest of my life.

CADENCE

It won't stop.

It's been one week since the pictures were printed.

One week of hiding.

One week of ignoring calls and emails and text messages.

One week of Sarah filtering any communication, and only letting the most important or absolutely ridiculous (for humor value) through.

One week of no Sebastian.

Might as well have been one whole week of no air.

But almost complete seclusion gives a person space, perhaps too much space, to think. And the thought I'm having right now is I've finally realized something GOOD that came out of having a sex tape released of me seven years ago.

It's that the second time around, I know what to expect.

The initial hysteria from family. Then the blame and humiliation. I've been sheltered from the scrutiny and judgment of strangers so far, but I know that's coming. But I'm already experiencing the support and love from those who matter.

And that's something I didn't know at the tender age of seventeen, that there are people who will matter, and there are those who just don't.

It's easy to brush off the words and opinions of complete strangers, but when it feels like the predominant social conscience has a particular view of you, it can be hard to overcome.

I don't know what the aftermath in terms of the media has been. Sarah decided that it would be better not to know, considering how I would burst into tears every time I came across a headline or saw the pictures in print again.

But I think it's time.

Time to get back to my life. And to start the process of moving on.

I thought the tears were for me, for my loss of privacy, for my past and present conspiring to ruin my life. But the tears were for the loss of something else. The loss of something so beautiful, that never really had the chance to become something real.

"Sarah?" I call out to my friend, who's never been more than a shout away.

"Yeah?"

"I think it's time for pizza."

She comes in, brushing her hair still wet from her shower. "Ok! You wanna order in? Or I can pick some up from the place downstairs?"

"No, let's go somewhere together."

"Out?"

"Yeah."

"You sure?"

"Yup."

She sits down on the bed in front of me and reaches out and squeezes my hand. I smile to reassure her, and thank her. For being the difference between me getting through this, and not.

She looks at me for a moment, making her judgment and I don't rush her. I owe her the right to make the decision, she earned it by being my shield for the last few days.

"Ok," she nods and gets up. "Just let me get changed."

SEBASTIAN

"Oh look, zombies do revert back to human form," Jez says as I come out of the bedroom, fully dressed for the first time in days.

"Hey," I say, and join them on the couch. "What's up?"

"Nothing much, just deciding where to go to grab a bite. You up for it?"

No. I'm not. But I wonder if I ever will be.

"Come on, man. How 'bout this, we just go across the road to the pub for a pint and a steak, an hour tops, and we'll get you back here before the bell dings."

"Fine."

"Great!" We all get up and grab our jackets.

"Guys." We turn to the door as Dennis walks in.

"Aw man, we were just going to go out for a bite."

"It'll have to wait."

"What's going on?"

"There's been, well, I've found out what happened with Sebastian and Cadence's pictures and, well, the others as well."

"Good! Drill that fucker to the ground!" Marius yells, swinging a right hook in the air.

"Shut up and sit down," our manager tells us, his voice hard and firm. Something's happened, something's happened and he's not happy about it.

"Dennis? What's going on, what'd you find out?" Jez presses him.

"Hey," a female voice speaks up quietly from the door.

It's Hailey.

"I need to tell you guys something."

Chapter Twenty-Five

CADENCE

"What the hell are you doing here?" Sarah demands when we return to the apartment to see Hailey standing there.

She takes a step towards me and I flinch, unconsciously backing up, seeking shelter behind my friend.

"Go," Sarah says to her, her voice angry, growing in volume.

"I have to speak to you," she says to me, ignoring Sarah. Her eyes are bloodshot and for a moment I can't help but liken them to my own.

Sarah can barely hide her agitation. "There's nothing you have to say to her, just go!"

"No, please, Cadence, just five minutes. I have to tell you what happened, and then I promise never to bother you again." Her voice cracks as she speaks. And I wonder what could have made it that way.

It physically hurts me to be this close to her, but a part of me craves information, yearns to know what happened and why. So, I just nod, and Sarah sighs.

I open the door and gesture for Hailey to follow us in.

"Have a seat," I gesture to a chair by the dining room table. Once she sits, I remind her, "Five minutes. And then I'm going to ask you to leave."

She nods. "Firstly, for everything that's happened, I'm sorry. I'm so, so sorry. I had no idea this was going to happen."

Sarah, who's standing behind me, scoffs, and I turn to shush her with a look.

"I had no idea she was interested in you guys, I just thought she was a groupie."

"Who? What are you talking about, Hailey?"

"Gemma, the girl who was with me that night at Patrick's club, do you remember? Do you remember her being with me?"

That night is such a blur to me, it takes some time for me to rifle through my memories to place a face to the name.

"She was the blonde girl who came with me to hang out at our booth," she adds and it helps to clear the fog.

"I remember her," Sarah mutters.

"That night, she said to me that you looked familiar to her, but she couldn't pick it. I didn't think anything of it. After that she kept trying to get me to find ways for her to hang out with the band, so I'd invite her out when we went out for drinks or something. Most of the time you and Sebastian weren't there. But the other night, when she found out about the concert, she practically begged for me to get her backstage. I thought she probably had a crush on Brad or Marius or something. Anyway, during the encore she talked me into going in to wait in the greenroom because surely everyone would go back there after the concert. That's when you guys came in. We didn't even have time to tell you we were there, so we just decided to hide out in the adjoining bathroom. I had NO idea she was filming, and no idea what she had planned. I guess the whole time she was just waiting for a chance to use the pictures that she had of you before. I guess she hit the jackpot. It was her, it was all her. I called her a few days ago and she admitted to everything. She even thanked me." Hailey stops and draws a long breath, shaking her head at her own words.

I can't believe what I'm hearing.

Literally.

I don't know if I can trust this woman standing in front of me who I've seen as my enemy for so long. Can I trust her with these revelations she's just dropped on me? I don't know what to say.

Sarah doesn't have the same restraint.

"I don't believe you," she says, narrowing her eyes.

Hailey turns to her, "I'm sorry, I don't know what else to tell you, but it's all true."

"I heard you that night, Hailey, in the bathroom, you were bragging about having slept with half the band and that you were going to try to score with Sebastian that night," Sarah accuses her.

The sound of his name makes me flinch and my breath catch. Images of him and her intertwined flash in my mind. I turn to Hailey and she looks at me, her jaw locked, speechless.

Then she takes a breath and closes her eyes.

"I lied. About all of it. None of that was true."

I stand up, facing her, the frustration taking a hold of me.

"So Gemma lied about being an undercover pap. Now you tell us you lied about fucking half the band. Maybe you're lying now, Hailey! What's the truth? What am I supposed to believe?"

"I'm not. I promise you, I'm not. I..."

"You're what, Hailey? You're going to have to give me something, or else you need to leave. Were you trying to score with Sebastian or not? Or is everything you've just told us to cover your own ass?"

"I'm GAY!" Hailey shouts and stands up, her eyes glistening, "I am gay," she repeats, her voice softer.

"What?" I stare at her.

"I have absolutely no interest in Seb or the band or any man for that matter. I am gay and I always have been."

And the revelations just keep coming. I sit back and watch her for a second. She's trembling and I wonder how many times she's had to tell someone what she's just told us.

"Do the guys know?" I ask.

"Yes. And they were sworn to secrecy. I've known them half my life...they know everything about me, and yes, they know I'm gay. And they know that it's up to me if I want someone to know or not."

And then it dawns on me.

"So, Sebastian..."

"Was just keeping his word to me."

"Even if..."

"Even if it meant losing you, yes."

The news doesn't make it any easier.

"But it was never about choosing between you and me. It was about keeping his word. He doesn't have anything if not his integrity. You should know that. But I can't do that to him. Keeping my secret can't be the reason that he loses you."

"But...why did you say all that stuff to Gemma?" Sarah comes up behind me, trying to find her own answers.

"I don't know. I guess I just felt like she was starting to get an inkling, and in some twisted way I wanted her to think I was cool. I haven't had a lot of female friends and I guess I just wanted her to like me. I had no idea that she was really just using me the whole time."

"Oh, Hailey." I can't help but feel for her. Living the life she does, mixing with famous people, never really knowing who to trust.

"I'm sorry, I'm so sorry. I'm sorry about the pictures, I'm sorry about you and Sebastian, but I'll do anything I can to fix it."

"You're...not in love with Sebastian?" I have to ask, one last time.

"No. I love him like a brother, like I do all of them, but nothing else."

"And you didn't have anything to do with the pictures?"

"Other than bringing that lowlife into our circle? No, I promise."

And I believe her.

"Okay."

"I'm sorry, Cadence."

"I believe you, Hailey. I accept your apology. I'm sorry it came to this."

"What's going to happen between you and Sebastian?" she asks after a few minutes of silence, as we all are lost in our thoughts.

"What do you mean? Nothing."

"This doesn't change anything?" Her question mirrors the one I've been asking myself.

"I don't know."

"He wasn't choosing between us, Cadence. He was choosing between keeping his word to me or not, and if you know anything about Seb, it's that he'll never break a promise to you."

"I think I know that much."

"And one more thing. It's that if you don't come back, he's never, ever going to be the same."

"Does he know you're here?"

"No. I've only just come from telling the guys what happened. They're not that happy with me either right now, for introducing Gemma to them. But well... Jez asked me to give you this." She holds out a small CD envelope to me.

I reach for it slowly, "What is it?"

"It's a recording of something he found on the computer. He thinks it's probably important you hear it."

SEBASTIAN

"So, what do you think?" Jez asks me once it's just to two of us left in the room. It's been a long day, and I just want some quiet time to myself.

"About what?"

"What Hailey told us."

"What is there to think? It happened, and now we know why. Dennis will do what he does." Though whatever that is, it'll only fix part of the problem. The rest is beyond fixing at this point.

"I mean about Cadence, what is this going to mean about you two?"

"Nothing. She already decided she wants nothing to do with me, what more can I do?" I try to answer him flippantly. I'm afraid of another shower intervention, if the boys catch me moping over my broken heart again.

"You could not be more of a chickenshit," Jez says to me, shaking his head.

"Hey."

"Seriously, man, where are your balls?"

"She doesn't want to see me. She hates me! She thinks it's me that did this to her and she blames Hailey, and in a way, she isn't wrong, even if it's not exactly how she thinks. What more can I do?"

"You make her realize that you're worth it, dude."

"I don't know if I can do that. Because I don't know that I DO deserve her."

"Well, duh! We all know you don't! But for some reason she's cockmad for you! Don't take that for granted."

I get up and wander over to the piano. Running my fingers over the keys, remembering the way she sat here, lost in the music, me watching her, mesmerized by her.

"What if I told you Hailey was over there explaining everything right now?" Jez breaks my daydream. "What if right now, Hailey was getting you off the hook?"

"I- I don't know! Does that change anything?"

"Goddammit, do I have to do EVERYTHING for you? DO you LOVE her, man?!"

"You know I do!"

"Then for fucking sakes, use those balls for something other than a toy to fiddle with when you're bored and go get your woman back!!"

CADENCE

I've waited as long as I can.

Waited until Hailey left and convinced Sarah to go home.

Waited until I took a shower and stood in the kitchen making tea and waiting for it to cool.

Waited until the sun had set and the stars had come out to play.

Waited until I could barely breathe from the weight of the suspense.

And now I'm ready.

I slide the CD into my laptop and click on the one file.

There's a soft buzz and then the sound of soft breathing in the microphone.

And then he speaks. "This is... this is "Cadence's Song". A song for my muse. My everything, my here, there, everywhere and in between. I miss you so much. This is for you."

My heart feels like it skips one, two, three beats and I thump myself on the chest to start it. The tears have already started to fill my eyes and I feel my fingers grip into fists, almost like I'm trying to capture the air particles that carry the timbres of his voice. How I've missed his voice. His words, his whispers into my shoulder as he cradles me from behind.

And then he starts to play.

It's a sweet, beautiful melody. Gentle and lilting, the sound of moonlight on water, of raindrops on skin. Parts of it sound so familiar, and I remember I've heard some of it before, heard it that night after the club incident.

It's him. It's all him. It's as though he's speaking to me, clearer than if he'd used words.

The song is heartbreaking, his notes long and sad, dark and yearning. It's like he's been watching me these last few days and turned my tears into music.

I feel so alone and yet so understood all at once.

I can't help but ponder what I've lost and what I may never find again. I'm not the same person I was when I was seventeen and shut my heart off to the world. Maybe this time, my response to the brutal invasion of my privacy should have been different. I tried exclusion, maybe this time I should've tried inclusion. Instead of hiding, I should've sought justice and strength in facing it together and publicly declaring, 'this is not acceptable'.

But it's too late. I cast the die in pain and fear.

The music ends on a tender, minor chord, the mournful sound of endings, and it fills my heart with an ache in the shape of him.

Chapter Twenty-Six

SEBASTIAN

"Will you fucking hurry up! You're going to make us late!" Jez yells from the hotel room door.

I pick up the last items left on the nightstand, tucking them into my pocket and look around the emptied hotel room.

I don't want to leave. I'm scared to. I'm afraid that the memories won't follow me, and when I close my eyes, I won't remember the first time she stood there, wringing her fingers trying to lay down conditions of our arrangement.

Or the night she'd laid like a broken doll in my bed and I'd realized I'd loved her and would protect her for the rest of her life if she'd let me.

Or the few happy days we had, after coming back from Uluru, making love over and over again on every surface of the suite, every look, every word of hers spiking the desire in me,

"SEBASTIAN! We're leaving RIGHT NOW!" Brad booms from the door and I know it's time to go. I close the bedroom door behind me and make my way to them.

"You ready?" Jez asks, and I know that I'm not.

But time doesn't stop for everyone and sometimes it's just time to take a leap.

CADENCE

The school decided to let me come back after three weeks when it seems the scandal has died down.

Working herself to the bone, Sarah did everything she could to take over my classes, knowing I'd feel more at ease with her in charge of my kids, feeling safe leaving them with her.

She called me every day to tell me that the kids were so angry at the school for making me take time off and could not wait for me to come back. That some of the parents had even come to speak on my behalf.

I admit that those calls and words gave me purpose. I spend the time off making revised lesson plans, trying to find more ways to inject fun and different learning techniques into the lessons. I had a renewed need to impart the love of music in my students, to teach them that we are so lucky to be gifted with music in our lives and to not take it for granted but to keep exploring more and more ways to bring it into your world. Music of all kinds and genres.

Now, at the end my first day back, I can't help but sink into my desk chair, exhausted. I'd forgotten when a full day of teaching could take out of you. I'm almost glad that we had to cancel orchestra rehearsal due to a clash in the schedule for most of the students.

"Miss Bray?"

A small voice calls my name and I turn to see Jenny, the orchestra's first violinist, standing in the doorway.

"Jenny! How are you?" I wave her in and she pauses, biting her lip.

I haven't had a chance to speak to her since she told me she had to quit orchestra and I had planned to arrange a meeting with her and her parents sometime next week. Seeing her makes me feel like I've been the most selfish teacher in the world, worrying about myself when I should've been caring for my students.

"Is everything okay, Jenny?"

"Yes, Miss Bray, I was just wondering, would you take a walk with me? I'm supposed to be at work, so I don't have a lot of time, but I wanted to talk to you about my music."

"Of course!" I slide my feet back into my shoes and get up, following her down the hallway.

"How are your parents doing, Jenny?"

"Actually, much better, Miss Bray. Things are still a little bit difficult at home, but we've had some help lately, that I think might help with me coming back to orchestra."

"That is wonderful!" I turn to her and smile and she returns it with a smile that warms my heart.

"Yes, it is. I just want to thank you, from the bottom of my heart. For everything you've done for me."

"I haven't done anything special, Jenny...just believed in you."

"No, you've done so much more than that...we are ALL so thankful to you. You are, I don't know what we would do without you."

And with those words, she pushes open school's front entrance doors, and there, in the front courtyard of the school is a huge crowd. Almost the size of the entire school! There are students and teachers, parents and admin staff. And everyone is facing me, and smiling and waving.

And I think my heart almost explodes with love in that moment.

Behind the crowd I can see a makeshift stage, and on it, my kids, my school orchestra, jumping up and down and screaming my name.

I turn to Jenny, speechless. Jenny just grins and runs up onto the stage and takes her place in the orchestra.

Sarah breaks from the group and comes up to hug me.

"Oh my god. What is this?"

She just smiles and points towards the stage. Everyone follows her lead and turns to see the principal standing there in front of the microphone.

"Miss Cadence Bray, the school orchestra, and I and everyone at the school want you to know how much we value and appreciate all that you have done to bring music into our school and hearts."

He waves to me and then turns toward the orchestra.

"I've waited so long to tell you this, it didn't feel right until your teacher was here, but Miss Bray singlehandedly raised over $50,000 for the school music program, which means that you will all be going to the Nationals this year in Canberra!"

I watch as the entire orchestra jumps up and starts screaming and hugging each other. I think my face almost splits from grinning with pride, I just want to run up there and join them.

Sarah, as always, can read my mind, and gives me a nudge. "Go! Go to them! You belong up there, this is your moment."

I run up through the crowd of people and up onto the stage, the kids running over and we all embrace in a great big group hug. I barely even notice the tears streaming down my face. I'd missed them so much the weeks I'd been away, worried about how they would feel about me when it was time to come back. Seeing them now, so happy, the worry and insecurity gone from their faces, it made it all worth it. I glance up at the sky for a moment and mouth a silent "Thank you, Sebastian." He and he only made this possible.

"And one more thing..." I hear Greg start to say and the kids suddenly all sit back down in their places, picking up their instruments. "The school orchestra now would like to thank Miss Bray and their parents with a special performance. Miss Bray, will you join me in your VIP seat?" He grins at me and points to a chair by the front of the stage.

I saunter over and give Greg a little pat on the arm, I can't help but feel more lighthearted than I have in weeks. The joy of my kids is contagious, and I just let myself become drunk in it.

I sit down and I watch as Timothy, one of the band leaders, comes to the front of the stage and takes up the conducting spot. He mimics me calling for silence and attention by doing a special wave of the conductor's baton and putting his index finger to his lips, and everyone who's seen me do it at the school performances laughs. He turns and winks at me and I poke me tongue out at him, secretly proud.

He lifts his arms and everyone is silent in anticipation.

And then they start to play.

From the first note, it's beautiful. This orchestra I've created from students who are here by the power of nothing but their own passion for music. It's so beautiful I just lose myself in it for a moment.

And then I realize, what they're playing it's a piece we've never practiced before.

But it's a piece I know like the beat of my own heart.

No. How can they.... no.

I shake my head, but the notes keep coming, sweet, simple, pure notes, like...I've said it before, like moonlight over water.

They're playing "Cadence's Song".

And just as my eyes draw tears from my aching heart, a giant cheer erupts from the crowd. I've heard that cheer before. I look up, my breath catching in my throat.

It's them. Jez, Marius, Brad.

But no Sebastian.

And my heart sinks.

I watch as the three members of the Rock Chamber Boys stop center stage, position their instruments and join in with the orchestra. Their parts ring out clear above the band, and even in my disappointment, I can't help but fall in love with their performance.

How had they even arranged to do this?

And how had they done it, without him?

And as if the gods have heard my question, the band and the orchestra fade away, and a single cello starts to play.

I search the stage, but he's not there.

And then I see him, standing alone in front of the stage in the grass. One man alone, but creating a symphony of sound just from his cello and his bow.

He's just like he was that first time I saw him on stage, eyes closed, hair over his face, lost in his own performance.

And just like that first time, he lifts his head and locks his eyes on mine.

I feel an explosion in my chest and I press my hand against my heart to stop it from breaking through my skin.

With the last few notes, I know. This song is mine, this man is mine and always will be.

The final note rings out and the crowd erupts into a chaotic applause.

I'm rooted to the spot and can't move. He smiles and reaches into his pocket and holds an object in his hand for a moment before throwing it up onto the stage at me. I reach out and grab it, gripping it tight, afraid to drop it.

I'm frozen and just keep staring at him. He doesn't move or say anything, his eyes dark and searching mine.

"What is it?" I hear a voice ring out, and it's Sarah, of course. I think everyone laughs, but I'm not sure.

I open my trembling hand. It's the rosin box. And all the memories come crashing back. I open the box and take out the little jar of rosin, wrapped in a little note.

I unwrap the note. And almost drop it.

"Marry me, maybe?" the clear black letters say.

Oh my god.

I look down to where he is standing, but he's not there. Panicked, I search the crowd but he's not there.

And then I feel a hand on the back of my neck. I spin around just as he drops to a knee. His hand reaches for the jar and he opens it, and like in a dream, pulls out a white gold diamond ring. He takes my hand and I can't help but notice how small mine looks cradled inside of his.

"Cadence," he says, I'm instantly dizzy from the sound of his voice saying my name. God, how I've missed it. "Marry me? I can't do this without you."

I look up into his eyes, and I wonder how I managed to get through the last three weeks without him.

"Do what?" I ask, already knowing my answer.

"Life."

Instantly, he looks hazy to me, and I realize I'm looking at him through tear-filled eyes. Happy tears because I know I'm about to be his forever.

"Yes," I say.

And now everyone knows it too.

He grins and slides the ring onto my finger and pulls me into his arms and kisses me. God, I've missed his kiss, the feel of my body fitting completely with his, the sweet salty taste of his lips. The way he moans when our tongues touch.

Suddenly, we hear the orchestra and the band break into the "Wedding March" and we pull apart and laugh. The crowd continues to cheer and we reward them with another kiss.

Finally, when the need for breath takes over, I pull away and whisper, "I love you, Sebastian."

"I love you, too, Cadence."

"How did you do all this?" I look around us, amazed that he could pull it all off. From the stage to the crowd to teaching the orchestra the song.

"Don't you know by now? I'm a romantic." He winks at me, and my knees do the wobble thing.

"You're a pain in my ass, more like! Why'd you wait so long?" I pout.

"I don't know, baby, I didn't know what I know now."

"What's that?"

"There's no living without you…"

I smile, before he continues, "Without you telling me what to do!"

"Hey!"

"Just kidding. I'm so sorry it took so long, I'll make it up to you." He tickles my ear with a kiss.

"I've heard that before." I poke my tongue out at him, and then yelp when he pinches my ass.

There's a squeal from the speaker and we turn to see Greg back at the microphone. He gives me a big thumbs up and I feel a surge of gratitude towards him for allowing all this.

He grabs the microphone from the stand and starts to address the crowd.

"Well, what a day! And would you believe, I have one last piece of news! I would also like to announce a brand-new music scholarship program we will have at the school, starting right now. Each year, one of the most gifted music students will have their music lessons and equipment paid for, they will have one-on-one mentoring with the some of the world's best musicians and will be invited to perform as their guest performer at one of their concerts – and this year, the inaugural recipient of our Rock Chamber Boys scholarship is JENNY YU!!!"

There's a squeal from the orchestra and we see Jenny jump up from her seat, screaming and covering her ecstatic face. She runs over to me, almost knocking Sebastian out the way and we jump up and down hugging each other tight. Finally, we calm down and I tell her, "I didn't do this. I think it's the band you need to thank."

She turns and just stares appreciatively at the band. "Thank you, thank you SO MUCH," she gushes.

Marius starts to turn red and brushes her thanks aside, grabbing his viola and yelling out, "Who's ready to PARTY!!"

The crowd screams and the boys break out into The Black-Eyed Peas' "Let's Get It Started" with the orchestra playing along.

I feel Sebastian pull me back against him, his face in my hair. I sigh. Wholly and completely happy.

"Did you do all this for me?" I wave my hand out over the stage and crowd.

"Yes. For you, for me, for music. For everything that matters to us."

"You're a big ol' softy, aren't you?" I turn, wrapping my arms around his neck.

"Yes, well...parts of me." He wiggles his eyebrows at me and I burst into a fit of giggles. "Other parts are big' ol' hard-y for you," he finishes, and suddenly, I want him so much I can't breathe.

"Oh, care to prove it?" I grin at him.

He pulls away me and leads me down the stage stairs. "You name the time and place, baby."

"First one back to the hotel gets first orgasm!" I challenge him, pulling away from him and heading for my car.

He stops and grips my hand, pulling me back into his arms, "Er, small change, I've moved out of the hotel."

"Wait, what?" I stop in my tracks, suddenly scared. "Where are you going?"

He smiles and presses a soft kiss to my forehead "I'm going home. With you."

Epilogue

SEBASTIAN

"Another round of applause for the Senior Orchestra from RedFern High School!"

The crowd's on their feet and I can barely make out the individual faces from my spot behind the curtain.

Cadence turns to the audience and bows and gestures to the orchestra who rise up onto their feet and take their bow. I'm clapping so hard I think I'm going to need to find a nurse's station for a wrist brace.

"THEY FUCKING KILLED IT!!" Brad jumps up and down next to me, punching his hands into the air and whooping with the best of them. We grin at each other proudly, as if we've had a part of it.

The kids file off the stage and into the backstage area where Marius and Jez greet them with hugs and high fives. Their faces are flushed and happy, still reeling from the excitement of their performance.

"Sebastian!" I turn at the sound of her voice and hold my arms out to catch her as she runs toward me.

"How were we???" Cadence asks me, her face no different to her students', flushed with excitement and pride.

"Fucking brilliant, that's how you were!" I tell her proudly, burying my face in her hair and taking a deep, deep breath of her heady orange blossom scent.

"Shhh! The kids!" She frowns at me for a moment, in response to my swearing, but the exuberance of performing breaks through like a streak of sunlight. I grin back at her, her joy for life always rubbing off on me.

"Oh shush, teach." I wink at her, and the kids around us giggle when she pokes her tongue out at me.

I look around us, at the 50 kids hopping with anticipation waiting for the final results of the National Orchestral Competition and I can't believe I could feel so connected to them after such a short amount of time.

These last few weeks in Australia after Cadence and I got engaged, we'd spent it in some sort of honeymoon like bliss, our time spent alternating between our bed, the recording studio and the school, the guys and I helping to get the orchestra into tip top shape for the competition. And now, seeing it all come together, it's even more nerve wracking than waiting for the envelope to open at the Grammys, we want these kids to win so bad!

"Ugh, Miss Bray, I think I'm going to throw up," Jenny moans, bent over a chair behind us.

"Are you ok, honey?" My fiancé runs over to her charge to check up on her.

"Ugh, yes, I'm just so nervous," the teenager moans again.

"Oh, I'm glad I'm not the only one," Marius pipes up, holding his stomach, "when are they going to make the damn announcement already?"

"I think…right now…" I point to the man in the suit walking across the stage with a sheet of paper in his hand.

The silence is deafening as we wait for him to clear his throat, tapping the microphone and making it squeal.

"After much deliberation, the judges have decided on the winner of this year's National High School Orchestral Competition. "

I feel a sharp pinch on my arm and I turn to see Cadence clutching me tight, her eyes squeezed tight in some sort of prayer. I can't help but feel my heart squeeze tight out of love for her in that moment, and I press a kiss to her forehead. Her eyelids flutter for a moment but stay closed and I turn my attention back to the stage.

"With their stunning performance of Tchaikovsky's Waltz of the Flowers and Cadence's Song, conducted by Miss Cadence Bray, the winner for the very first time, is Redfern High School from Sydney!!!"

There's a stunned silence around me, but just for a moment, and then the elation erupts and all I can see and hear are arms and happy faces and tears and hugs breaking out around me.

I can't stop grinning as the kids flood the stage pulling my beautiful fiancé on with them as they practically snatch the trophy out of the MC's hands, waving to the audience filled with proud family members who've traveled all this way to watch them.

"Good work, man," I feel a pat on my back and I nod.

"You too, Jez," I smile at my band mate, knowing he was as invested in them as I was. "Hey, thanks for, you know, helping me out with it all."

A wolfish grin spreads across Jez's face. "Man, don't be going soft on me now, save that for your woman."

"Oh, he's never gone soft on me, Jez," Cadence's voice speaks up behind us, and we realize she's left the stage to join us, "Just the opposite in fact." She winks at me, and instantly I wonder if there's anywhere we can find a moment to be by ourselves.

Jez just shakes his head and walks off, high fiving Brad as he goes.

"Why, Mary, whatever did you mean by that?" I pull her in close and nuzzle my face against her neck.

She laughs and pulls away, glaring at me for a moment, "You know, you never did tell me why you call me that."

"You still haven't figured it out after all this time?"

"I'm almost afraid to now."

"Mary. For Mary Poppins!" I finally admit and her mouth falls open.

"Dear lord, why on earth, why?"

"Because your first impression of her is that she's strict and cold, but as you get to know her, you find out, she's caring and thoughtful, loves the children to the end of the world and back even though she knows one day they won't need her any more. Oh, and under that highly buttoned collar, she's sexy as all hell."

Cadence lets her head fall back in a loud laugh, but the sparkle in her eyes tells me she probably won't mind me calling her by her nickname anymore.

"And you knew all that about me after only 30 seconds?" She looks up at me with those full, round, brown eyes.

"A man can hope." I wink.

"So, where to now?" Jez comes up to us, draping his arms around our shoulders

"What do you mean? I thought you never wanted to leave Australia?" I remind him.

"Well, er...you know, sometimes it's better to leave them wanting more...and me wanting to be far, far away from them."

"I knew it! I told you." I give him a soft slap on the back of his head and he pouts and rubs it.

"Well, you can go wherever it is you want to go," Dennis contributes, "As long as it ends up in London in two weeks. That's when the launch of your publicity tour for the new album starts."

I push Jez out of the way and grab Cadence by the wrist and twirl her into my arms.

"How 'bout it? What are you doing for the next few weeks?" I ask her.

"School's out for summer, so I'm all yours."

"A month of tea and biscuits it is!"

"And kisses?" She looks up at me, with that look that is both sweet and unbearably sexy.

"Yeah." I brush her eyebrow with my lips.

"Then I don't care where we are, as long as I'm with you."

"Always, babe. It's you and me, forever. Here, there, everywhere and in between."

~*~

Here is the end of Play Me, Sebastian and Cadence's story.
Read on for a preview to STRUM ME,
Brad's steamy hot second chance romance!
You'll get a glimpse into what Sebastian and Cadence
are up to as well.

STRUM ME

BRAD

"*Definitely* lobster."

They're the first words I hear when I open my eyes.

"I dunno...more like a cherry tomato?" another voice suggests from somewhere to the right of me.

"Nah, that doesn't really describe the dry, crusty, beef jerky value of it. I'm going with...hmmm, a rare prime rib roast left out in the desert for three days," a third person pipes up in a French accent.

"Oooh yeah, that's a good one! I changed my mind, I'm going with that!" says the lobster commenter's voice.

"What the fuck are you idiots talking about?" I finally break in, my shoulders cracking as I raise them over my head in a long stretch, pulling them out of my deep sleep.

"We're talking about the right side of your face, tit-wad," Sebastian, the owner of the French accent helpfully informs me.

My hand immediately goes to my right cheek.

"Oww!" My fingers snap back as my cheek tightens in a sharp pain. "What the?" I scan my brain for the reason for the pain.

"Roast beef jerky talking! That'll teach you to fall asleep next to an open window for a twelve-hour flight! We've been chasing the sun the whole time...and it looks like your ugly mug caught it!" Sebastian manages to get out before falling off his chair in laughter.

I push myself up out of my leather recliner and run to the little bathroom on our private plane.

They're right; my face is a blazing, blistering red—that is, until it comes to the bridge of my nose. Down the other side of the slope it's still a pasty white. I look like hell's version of the phantom from *Phantom of the Opera*.

"Ugh, fuck, you couldn't pull the blind down for me?" I grumble as I return to my seat, deliberately knocking my elbow against Marius's head as I pass him doing one of his yoga poses in the spacious lounge area next to the recliners.

Plopping my ass down into my seat, I dab a cold-water towel against my sore cheek.

"Ow. Ball-breath!" Marius shouts, losing his balance and toppling over into a pile of arms and legs.

"Hey, it's not our fault that after two weeks under the glaring Australia sun you still had the complexion of a prebaked loaf of bread," Jez says as he comes over, pushing his face close up to get a better look at my enraged skin, poking at it gently with his finger.

"Well, I guess I didn't get as much sun as you guys did," I explain as I swat Jez away.

"True. There wasn't much sun in that pool house with...what was her name again?" Sebastian goads me.

"Hollie," Marius shouts.

"Jenny," Jez follows.

"Karli!" Sebastian gleefully finishes off.

"All of those and more." I poke my tongue out at my bandmates. This wasn't going to be a discussion I was going to get out of looking good. Time to deflect. "Hey, I'm not the only one leaving the sunny gold coast of Australia without a tan. What about Sebastian? Did you and Cadey come up for food or oxygen even once?" I'm referring to Cadence, his newly acquired fiancée and our sometime-bandmate.

"Hey. Our love *is* our air," Sebastian waxes poetic, then grins as I make a puking noise, sticking a finger down my throat. "You say that now, but one of these days you're going to meet your own Cadence and knowing you, we're all going to be projectile vomiting before you know it."

"Fat chance, dude. My whole body will be as shriveled up as that beef jerky you so sweetly described my face as, before I'm going to get caught by a woman. I already learned that lesson a long time ago."

"Famous last words, buddy," he replies and I shiver a little at the thought that he might be right.

"What the fuck is that?!" a loud voice booms from the back of the plane and we spin our chairs around to see our long-suffering manager, Dennis, coming toward us. He comes to a stop next to me and jabs a finger in the direction of my face. Dennis is not a nuanced man, and it's usually pretty easy to tell from the look on his face when he's not happy with us. Probably because we've had so much practice at seeing it. Kind of like...right now.

"Um...what's he talking about?" I whisper through the side of my mouth to the other guys.

"Oh, I think he's referring to your face's impression of a red and white yin and yang figure," Marius answers unhelpfully.

"WHAT IN GOD'S UNHOLY EARTH HAPPENED TO YOUR FUCKING FACE?" Dennis finally booms by way of an answer.

"What? Oh this? It's just a little bit of sunburn. No biggie." I try not to cringe as my fingers graze over the tender skin of my cheek.

"You look so fucking ridiculous! We have a press conference as soon as we land! You know the only reason you pickle-dicks are famous at all is because you all look like you belong on the cover of magazines, right? And I DON'T mean *Dermatology Today*! FUCK ME!" He glares at me and I shrink a little into my seat.

"Hey! That hurts our feelings. We're famous because we're talented, right guys?" I implore the guys to take a little of the heat off me.

"Uhmmnowesuckwe'rejustpretty.ThanksforeverythingDenniswe loveyouuuuuu," the three of them mumble and pretend to be suddenly engrossed in their newspapers and fingernails. Wuss-asses.

"And um, why did you book our flight so close to our press conference time anyway?" As soon as the words leave my mouth I wish I can take them back. "Um, never mind."

Dennis's face quickly burns a bright red, not too different to the right side of my own face. He takes a deep breath and I can feel it coming. "Why? Why?? WHY DID I BOOK YOUR FLIGHT SO LATE?"

"Er, no, it's okay. I'll forgive you this time." I try to spin my chair away from the wrath that is coming, but I feel it stop in its tracks and the chair spin back around to face my manager.

"Oh, maybe you didn't realize, I DIDN'T book your flights to London so close to your press conference time. In fact, the plane is a WHOLE DAY late because...someone... SOMEONE arrived six hours late to the airport and we missed our window for takeoff and had to wait a WHOLE DAY later to leave. Someone...SOMEONE...Who could that have been, I wonder?" At this point his face is way redder than mine and his two bunched-up fists tell me, he's not finding this as funny as the three smirking faces behind him.

I decide the best way to handle it is to just sit completely still, play...not quite dead, just spontaneously comatose, and then maybe the beast will just give me a few sniffs and wander off.

So, for just a moment, I don't move and avoid eye contact. I can hear his hissing breath easing and as I predicted, one of the other thousands of problems we cause him distracts him and he swings around and glares at Sebastian.

"And YOU!" Dennis points to my ill-fated bandmate.

"AH!! What did I do?" Seb jumps out of his skin and narrows his eyes at me.

"Where is Cadence?"

"Um, she's in Sydney. Did it take twelve hours for you to notice she's not here?"

"Where is she? I thought she was coming with us. They're expecting her as well."

"She's coming in a few days; she just had to finish up some work and then she can enjoy the rest of her summer with us instead of worrying about her students." Sebastian explains. Cadence is a music teacher at a local school, and until very recently when a sexy French cellist stole her heart, the school and her students were her life.

"But they're going to be expecting her to get off the plane with us. The stories are going to run rampant about you guys breaking up if you arrive alone."

The sound of the four of us guffawing stuns Dennis out of his grump.

"Denny, after what they've been through, I think 'breaking up' is hardly the news headline that's going to bother Cadence at this point," Marius finally speaks up, referring to the recent sex video scandal headlines in the international media that almost broke them up.

Dennis sighs and sinks into an empty recliner, the guilt of not being able to stop the scandal still weighing heavily on him, and Sebastian gets up to pat him on the shoulder.

"Take it easy old man, or you're going to give yourself a heart attack."

Jez follows and hands Dennis a drink, who takes a sip and hisses, the amber liquid probably burning his throat.

"And don't worry about Brad's face. It actually is an improvement. You know he's always been the ugliest one out of all of us."

This gets a chuckle out of Dennis and he gives me a limp smile. "Yeah, I guess. Just...try to sit with your less ugly side to the cameras, will you? With this one," his head gestures to Sebastian, "out of play, we need the rest of you to be pulling your dreamboat status weight."

I sigh and stand up and wrap my arms around Dennis' shoulder in a man hug that he only mildly struggles to get out of.

"Keeping the ladies happy? I can do that, Dennis, just for you."

I'm too busy patting myself on the shoulder to see the fist coming toward my face.

***

The pounding in my head is somewhere about eight on the migraine Richter scale.

The twelve hours of sleep I got on the plane barely made up for the sleep I'd missed out on partying in Australia for two weeks. Now the jetlag and the two cans of Red Bull are doing a tango on the nerve behind my left eye. That's on top of the way the right side of my face screams every time I inadvertently make some sort of facial expression.

And it'd all be okay if I were headed for a nice, dark room and into a soft, warm bed. Instead, there are about a hundred of London's most zealous music journalists and paparazzi on the other side of the door, ready with their microphones and flashbulbs and wanting blood.

"You guys ready?" Dennis asks us for the eighteenth time since he herded us into the hotel bathroom to give us his best pep talk on how important these press tours were to the success of the launch of our new album. I'd like to think he didn't turn toward me when he'd said, "Well, just don't, you know, FUCK UP," but I know better.

"He means you," Jez clarifies, without needing to.

I am notoriously bad at these things and usually walk the tightrope between saying completely ridiculous nonsense and clamming up all together. If there's something I've learned about being in the public eye for the last eight years, it's that there are some born for celebrity and schmoozing the press, like

Sebastian and Jez, who can charm the horns off an angry bull. And then there are the ones like me, and to a lesser extent, Marius, who turn into gibberish-speaking spider monkeys at the mere sight of a microphone.

"He knows. Get off his case. He already looks white as a ghost… well, a ghost with sunburn." Seb defends me, patting me gently on the arm.

I give him a thankful smile that quickly turns into a cringe as my forehead threatens to tear from my cheek.

Rubbing my temples, I drag breath into my lungs, trying to stop the thumping against my skull and will my headache away. It's going to be a rough hour.

"You're up, guys." Dennis pats me on the back and it's one of those rare times I wonder why I'm doing this. Then I feel myself pulled into a big group hug, my bandmates' arms wrapped around my shoulder and our four faces in a huddle. These are the faces I've grown up with, gone through hell and back with, achieved the highest level of success with, faces I would die for, and then I remember. I'd be completely lost without them, doing what I love with the people I love most in the word.

Dennis gives us a wink and pushes the door open and there's a loud cheer and applause.

Marius steps onto the stage first and takes a seat behind the long table, followed by Jez and then Sebastian. I hang back watching them from the doorway, wondering who would notice if I made a run for it.

"Go!" Dennis whispers and gives me a little shove and I reluctantly follow my bandmates into the ring of fire.

The applause dies down as we settle into our seats and adjust the microphones in front of our faces.

I see Dennis nod to us and then Hailey, our new PR rep and Dennis's daughter, walks onto the stage with her own microphone.

"Welcome, everyone, and on behalf of the Rock Chamber Boys, I'd like to thank you all for being here today! We are so proud to announce the release of the new album, due next wêk, *Chords and Chaos*, and believe it's the best one yet. We'll be here for the next hour taking any questions…so let's start!"

An ocean of hands rise up and I see Hailey point to someone in the crowd.

"Hey guys, welcome back to London," a small lanky guy in a leather jacket stands up and addresses us. He looks familiar, but then again, they all do. We've done the rounds so many times, there aren't many journalists we haven't come across at one time or another. I just can't remember the good ones from the bad ones. "Congrats on the new album, it's great," he continues. "But, just wondering, why did you guys change your name?"

There's a twittering among the crowd and I guess a few people are wondering the same thing, even though we'd released a memo when we recently changed it.

We all turn to Sebastian, who is probably the best one to answer, and he just grins and leans into the microphone as if it's not an instrument of evil.

"Hey Gil, nice to see you again, man," he starts. Gil! That's it! Ugh, how the hell does he remember these names? Not for the first time I can't help but be in awe of my bandmate and his social adeptness. "Well, as you know, we'd been No Strings Attached for the last eight years, but a lot has changed in that time. From our style of music to band members coming and going. But we really feel like we've reached a certain stage in our music careers where we needed to make a change, to mark where we are now. And Rock Chamber Boys seemed like the perfect name to describe what we are—a contemporary music outfit that also combines the incomparable classic string instrument chamber music of centuries before us. We like it, so we hope you guys do too. But frankly, Gil, we don't give a damn." He finishes with a grin and wink.

And they eat it all up.

The next half an hour flies by pretty quickly, and I don't talk too much, only once in a while when we see Dennis gesture to me and I interject with a quick jib or two just to prove I'm not completely mute. But for most of the time I'm happy to sit back and let Jez and Seb spin their web while I sit there behind my shades, pretending to appear mysterious. It's a role I've perfected and prefer, and find that the few times I *do* speak, they tend to pay attention more.

A loud laugh from the crowd jolts me out of my daydream of going back to the hotel room for a long hot soak in the tub.

Leaning over to Sebastian, I nudge him and whisper, "What happened?"

He grins and whispers back, "Jez just tried to hit on that blonde pap over there and she told him she only dates guys who wear less eyeliner than she does."

I can't help but guffaw as I look over and see Jez is still pouting. His pride in his hairstyles and "face styles" as he calls them, is well known to anyone who knows anything about the band. His pout quickly breaks out into a grin however, and he shrugs and holds his hands out in defeat.

"Okay, okay, enough picking on Jez," Hailey jokes into the microphone, before glancing at Dennis who twirls his finger, in the universal "wrap it up" gesture. "I think we have time for one more question before we let these guys grab some sleep. They have just come off a plane from Sydney after all. So…yes, you, the young lady in the back, what question have you got for the band?"

There's a squeaking of the chair legs scraping against the floor and everyone turns to the back of the room, toward the sound. The lights, as always, are shining directly into our eyes and I try to block them out with my hand, looking out into the crowd. I see a female silhouette stand up, with long dark hair, but I can't make out anything else about her.

Until she speaks.

"Yeah, um, I just have one question: do you guys ever intend on doing anything but ripping off other musicians' work?"

There's a smattering of murmurs and Sebastian spits out his water next to me.

But it's not the question that has my heart skipping a beat.

It's the voice.

It's hers.

It could only ever be hers.

Butter.

Strum Me, book 2 in the Rock Chamber Boys series.

Available on Amazon and FREE on Kindle Unlimited.

Also available soon on audiobook at audible.

About the Author

First thing about the author you should know is, she hates writing these "About the Author" things.

But if you should run into her in a café in her hometown of Adelaide, Australia, then for the price of a free smile, she'll tell you details you never needed to hear about another person.

Her husband can vouch for this. It's how they met. Kinda. But you'll hear all about that when you run into her in a café in Adelaide.

She hopes you liked her book though. Like, really. It's pretty much all she's ever wanted to do. Write a book that you'd want to read.

Thanks for helping to fulfil that dream.

Also by Daisy Allen

Available on Amazon and Kindle Unlimited and Audible

<u>The Rock Chamber Boys Series</u>
Play Me: Book One.[1]
Strum Me: Book Two.[2]
Serenade Me: Book [3]**Three.**
Rock Me: Book Four
<u>Men of Gotham Series</u>
Kaine[4]
Xavier
<u>An O'Reilly Clan Novel</u>
Once Bitten[5]

***

Please subscribe to Daisy Allen's email newsletter to receive information on upcoming new releases and bonus offers just for subscribers!

http://www.subscribepage.com/b3l2q9

---

1. https://www.amazon.com/dp/B073TS92R9
2. https://www.amazon.com/gp/product/B078W9ZSZ8
3. https://www.amazon.com/gp/product/B07JHBKKHB/ref=series_rw_dp_sw
4. https://www.amazon.com/gp/product/B079Y9RG7Y/
5. https://www.amazon.com/dp/B06Y444Q8Q

You can also follow Daisy on Facebook for ramblings and extras: **facebook.com/daibyday/**

Made in the USA
Middletown, DE
28 October 2022